The Elephant Gate

The True Story of Siam, Berlin's Last Elephant

Curtis Christopher Comer

I meant what I said, I said what I meant. An elephant's faithful, one-hundred percent.

Dr. Seuss, "Horton Hears a Who"

The Elephant Gate

1943

The elephant stood motionless among the chaos. Even as deadly ordnance rained from the heavens, obliterating everything around him, killing, maiming, burning, he stood as if chained to a tree. Animals in surrounding enclosures shrieked in terror as explosion after explosion shook the sandy ground, their cries filling the air like some grotesque death chorus, accompanied by the whistle of the falling hell. Walls around the elephant crumbled and fell, roofs were blown heavenwards, and bits of concrete and tile pelted his tough skin but he remained, unmoving. His cell mate had bolted from their enclosure as soon as a hole opened in the wall and he had the urge to run, too, but he couldn't leave her, even as the fire to his back singed the coarse hairs on his back and tail. No, he couldn't leave her. He had promised her that much.

The light from the fires in the surrounding buildings reflected in the twenty-two year old elephant's eyes and the thick smoke stung his sensitive trunk. He could taste blood, which was oozing from his left ear, no doubt caused by the explosion that had destroyed his enclosure. The earth trembled beneath his massive hulk, more subtle than an earthquake, but far more deadly on that cold November night turned into hell.

Suddenly a giraffe, freed from its enclosure, bolted past, in search of safety. It disappeared in a flash and tears filled the elephant's eyes when he again spied the giraffe, this time motionless on the ground.

Humans, just as confused as their animal charges, darted here and there in an attempt to avoid the catastrophe they had created. The elephant wanted to kill them, to make them pay for what they had done to her and for what they had done to his mother.

His mother.

It had already been twenty-two years since the death of his mother, but he still remembered that day, an elephant always remembers. He could still hear his mother's voice, telling him the story of the creation and of the goddess. Back then he had been known as Da-ra, before the humans changed his name.

Standing amid the chaos of war, among the burning buildings and dying animals, the elephant's thoughts drifted back to the jungles of his homeland, back to the time before.

Chapter One

At the beginning of the all that is the goddess, Ha, was.

It is her name that all living creatures, whether they slither across the dirt or soar freely across the heavens, speak at the moment of birth and at the very last moment of life, the sound of Her entering or leaving the body.

Ha existed, happily living among the stars until, one day, she realized that she was lonely. Without pain or effort she gave birth to the god, Phi-ra. Seeing the beauty of her creation, she mated with the young god and became pregnant with their child. Ha knew, however, that their offspring would need a place to live and so she created the earth with its jungles, forests, lakes and oceans. She saw her creations and they were good, and so she gave birth to her baby, Gro, the first elephant. For a thousand years all was well, and Ha taught her child the mysteries of the universe, blessing her with an excellent memory and the virtue of loyalty. Phi-ra, meantime, had grown jealous of the attention shown by his mother-consort to his sister-daughter. In a rage, he tricked Gro into eating the fruit of the Pangi bush, which killed her. Ha was so angered by the death of her daughter, Gro that she banished Phi-ra to the daytime sky, nevermore to return to the earth. In his exile, the god became a god of fire, destroyer of world and lord of the warm months, spewing fire from his erect trunk.

Then a strange thing happened; as Gro's body decayed, it became part of the earth and from this new earth sprang more elephants, herd after herd after herd.

Ha saw this and was very happy. So that the children of Gro would not be lonely, Ha created hippopotamus', rhinoceroses, monkeys and birds. She knew that balance was necessary to this arrangement, so she created lions and tigers, too, as well as zebras and camels and cows. Ever mindful of Phi-ra's treachery, Ha mandated that, from that point on, all bulls must leave the female herds at musth, the time of sexual awakening.

Because she couldn't bear to leave her creations without protection and fearing that Phi-ra might plot his revenge, Ha decided to keep watch over them from the cover of the nighttime sky, where she remains cloaked, one of her eyes, luminous and white, watching her children from the heavens. There she remains as mother protector and lady of the cold months.

It has been a millennia since the banishment of Phi-ra and the self exile of Ha but, each day and night, the god and goddess conduct their cautious dance in the sky, wheeling and spinning about the heavens, each taking their turn watching the earth.

The bull calf, barely three years old, followed his mother closely through the high grass and listened to her stories of the goddess, Ha. Since nothing was written down, these stories were passed on orally, from generation to generation, mother to daughter, mother to son and so forth. The calf's three aunts and two sisters, the other members of the herd, carefully surrounded him, all on the look-out for rogue tigers, which might be tempted by his size and vulnerability. They hurried him along and took extra care not to step on him in their haste. The calf was the only male in the herd and, when he was old enough, he would be compelled to leave the safety of the females and join an all-male bachelor herd, which was elephant custom, as mandated from the beginning of time. For now, though, he would remain among the females, under the protection of his mother, sisters and aunts. His mother, Su-ha, was the matriarch of the herd and she dutifully led her charges to food and water, the knowledge of their locations locked within her memory from years of practice.

As was elephant custom, the latter half of her name, as with all females, was taken from the name of the goddess. Males, in turn, shared the name of the god, Phi-ra. Therefore, the young bull was called Da-ra.

The rainy season was quickly approaching and, as was their habit, the herd would soon relocate to the safety of the trees where food and water would be plentiful and where human hunters were less likely to harass them. The young bull, Da-ra, had only seen humans once, at a distance, but had thought it strange how they walked on two legs like the monkeys he had seen in the jungle. He had imagined that such constant posturing must have been tiring, an assumption that neither his mother nor aunts bothered to contradict. He did know, however, that not all humans were bad. Some, in fact, held elephants in very high regard and would venture into the jungles during their festivals with food for the wild elephants. Da-ra even recalled his mother, visited by these kind humans, decorated with flowers and painted with the symbol of Phi-ra, the sun god, an equal armed cross, with hooks coming off of each arm. This interaction with humans was something the older elephants tolerated in exchange for the gift of food. Otherwise, Su-ha told her son, it was best to keep away from them. Their erratic nature and seeming lack of memory made them too unpredictable.

Su-ha was thirty years old and massive in size for a female. Her right tusk was shorter than the left, caused by years of using it to dig in the dry dirt for water and roots. She had learned all she knew from her mother and grandmother. She had learned for instance, where to find the best watering holes, sometimes as much as fifty miles away, which fruits to eat and which ones to avoid. She learned that, in the dry season, when Phi-ra takes revenge by drying up watering holes, there is always more water to be found if only by digging for the water hidden by the goddess and that, even with ground vegetation gone, there was still plenty of food to be had in the trees. She learned, too, the location of the place of eternal sleep, the resting grounds of the ancestors, deep within the jungles. She knew that this place, littered with the bones of the ancestors, was where she, too, would go one day. Da-ra remembered quite well the day his grandmother, the original matriarch of the herd, had ventured off in search of the place of eternal rest. As she said her goodbyes, she consoled her grandson with words he could not yet comprehend.

"Do not cry, child," she had said, "one day you will see me again, not in the place of eternal rest but in the place after."

Although he had been quite young, he clearly remembered joining in mourning with the rest of the herd.

Su-ha promised her young calf, the youngest of her three offspring, that she would take him there one day so that he could learn of its mysteries. For now, though, he would have to settle for her descriptions of the place.

***

The herd had spent much of the dry season in the low country, feeding on grasses and trees and did their best to avoid the humans who occasionally wandered into their territory. One of Da-ra's sisters, Mo-ha, had been recently impregnated by a bull from a neighboring bachelor herd. Although they knew that it would be nearly two seasons before the birth of the baby growing inside of her, the other females fussed over her as if she was carrying the next Phi-ra in her belly. Their progress was slow, and not only because of the pregnant Mo-ha or the young bull who struggled to keep pace. One of Da-ra's aunts, nearly forty years old, had stepped on a sharp bit of stump, which had been felled by one of the destructive humans, and her foot was swollen and painful to step on. As a result, the rest of the herd adjusted their pace so that she could keep up. As they neared a rise, however, the matriarch stopped in her tracks. Just a few yards ahead and directly in their path, there were humans. Some, the darker skinned ones, sat astride captive elephants while the others, pale skinned with light hair, sat in their rolling machines. Su-ha lifted her trunk and sniffed the humid air while the herd stood, frozen, behind her. Of the herd, it was only Da-ra, filled with youthful curiosity, which joined his mother's side. He peered from behind the safety of one of her massive legs as Su-ha raised her head and fanned her ears to show the humans that she refused to be hindered on her journey. Still, with her young calf, a pregnant daughter and a wounded sister she felt that caution was the only logical course of action. Warily, she changed direction, heading back in the direction they had just come. If they walked back two miles and then cut across the grass, she reasoned, they would be to the cover of the jungle before sundown. The herd, which showed no sign of panic, despite the fact that they were aware of the danger, dutifully followed the matriarch. Da-ra, close by his mother, glanced back at the humans who, amazingly, sat unmoving in their machines. He breathlessly inquired of the elephants he had seen, the ones with the humans and his mother explained, her voice tinged with sadness, that they were slaves and not to be blamed for their actions. The humans, she explained, beat captive elephants until all elephant behavior was gone from them. As a result, the slave elephants did their master's bidding for fear of more beatings. Su-ha knew that the slave elephants were also used to run down any elephants that might make it to the safety of the trees, but kept this from her young son. She ignored Da-ra's barrage of further questions on the matter. With the humans so nearby, she knew that they could not waste a single minute.

***

It was nearly sundown by the time Su-ha decided that it was again safe to head east, in the direction of the jungle. In fact, she could see the lush canopy from the trail and the herd followed her as she stepped into the high grass. Da-ra's aunt, Sa-ha, pressed close to the young bull. She knew the dangers that lurked in the high grasses. Even mature elephants were known to have been attacked by tigers in such places and she was determined to protect her nephew, no matter the danger to her. Suddenly, a sound worse than any tiger filled the air and the herd froze in terror. Su-ha raised her right leg and fanned her ears in an effort to identify the terrible sound. Her sisters did the same, their ears like a sea of palm leaves. Horrified, Su-ha could see the humans, riding in their rolling machines and on the backs of the slave elephants, quickly approaching from the left. She knew that there was little chance of outrunning them---especially with her wounded sister---but she knew that they had to at least try. She signaled to the herd to run for the trees and they took off at a gallop, heading in the direction of the lush jungle.

The humans easily caught up to them and the first shot pierced the humid air like a clap of thunder. This was followed by the shrieks of the birds in nearby trees. Su-ha suddenly stopped, dazed. Da-ra watched in amazement as his mother dropped onto her knees, her torso still defiantly in the air. As was elephant custom, the herd gathered around her, undeterred in the face of the attacking humans. Da-ra stood in front of his wounded mother and was shocked to see blood oozing from the side of her face. Her eyes were already beginning to cloud over but she reached down and wrapped her trunk protectively around her calf. Da-ra started at the sound of another shot and another and another. He wanted to bolt, to continue running for the trees, but could not, encircled by his aunts. The ground around him shook as his aunts and sisters hit the ground, their screams maddening to the young, confused bull. Still, he was protected within the circled herd, their bodies like mountains surrounding the blood soaked valley in which he stood.

When the shooting finally stopped he realized that his aunts were only protecting him with their dead bodies. His mother, still not dead, continued to hold him with her trunk and tears filled her eyes.

> "Never forget," she said, her breath growing suddenly shallow. "Never forget all I have told you."

Terrified, Da-ra blurted,

> "But how do I find the place of eternal sleep?"
>
> "Remember," replied Su-ha, "it is in the jungle in the place of water. When it is your turn you will find me there and then in the place after."

A pale-skinned human, with hair the color of dried grass and holding a long object, appeared, having climbed on top of the body of his pregnant sister. He showed his teeth to Da-ra and said something to another human, who had appeared behind him. Su-ha pushed her calf to one side and lunged at the humans, knocking the first to the ground with a swipe of her massive trunk. The second human, as pale as the first and holding a similar long object, raised it to his shoulder and pointed it at the injured cow. A final shot felled Su-ha and she fell limply to one side, shaking the ground with her massive frame. A sound like a tree full of parrots filled the air and the first man, who had arisen from the bloody ground re-approached, still showing his teeth. He said something to the men outside of the ring of carcasses before abruptly turning, leaving the baby elephant alone.

Da-ra trembled and looked at his mother, who appeared to be sleeping. How could she ever reach the place of eternal sleep now? His thoughts were interrupted by the dark-skinned humans who suddenly appeared, holding large knives, similar to the ones he had seen them use to cut fruit from high in the palm trees. When they began hacking at his dead sisters and aunts Da-ra let out an anguished scream. Trunks were hacked off along with tusks, ears and feet. Stomachs were pried open and the contents leaked onto the parched ground.

His sister's dead baby was pulled from her stomach and tossed onto the grass. Da-ra wanted to run but he felt dizzy, barely able to stand.

The tranquilizer dart that was suddenly and unceremoniously shot into Da-ra's body was an unexpected blessing, as if sent by the goddess herself.

Chapter Two

1933

Da-ra, now called Siam by the humans, swayed uneasily in his wooden crate as the lorry onto which it was loaded changed gears to navigate an incline in the road. He leaned forward, placing all of his weight on his front leg in an effort to stabilize himself, and pressed an eye to a gap between two of the wooden planks, trying to get an idea of his surroundings. The light outside was bright, Phi-ra's golden disc in the sky not quite overhead, and he blinked a couple of times before his eye could adjust to the light. He could see that he was on a wide boulevard alive with activity. People hurried along the sidewalks like ants, carrying boxes and satchels and their young, and more rolling machines like the one he was riding on zipped past, belching their foul-smelling fumes into the air. Occasionally the rolling machines emitted noises not unlike the noise of a young elephant, something Siam had first noticed right after his capture, and it had been his instinct to answer them, although he had since learned better. As the lorry moved along, Siam kept redistributing his weight in order to maintain his balance, peering out of his crate at the passing scenery.

Hanging at intervals on poles along the wide boulevard were gigantic red banners that waved in the slight summer breeze, the same banners that he had seen in Munich, with the white circle in the middle and the twisted black cross in the middle of that. Although elephants do not see color in the same way that humans do, they are able to differentiate between hues, and so Siam knew that the banners were red. The black cross was similar to the crosses of Phi-ra, like the humans had once painted on his mother during festivals back in the jungle, and they made him homesick. Not that he would ever see his mother again, this he knew. The ruthless men who had captured him had shot her when she tried to protect him. It was their way, just as it had been his mother's instinct to protect her child. And, in the honorable tradition of never abandoning an injured matriarch, it had been his aunt's and sister's instincts to remain at her side, though it inevitably led to their deaths, too. It was surely a boon for the poachers that fateful day.

Although nine years had already passed since he had been taken, Siam still harbored a deep hatred for his captors. After watching the humans chop up his mother and aunts, taking tusks and feet and flesh, he had been tied to a tree without food for a week. He was then placed in a large crate and onto a rolling machine. The rolling machine took him to the water, and Da-ra was transferred a very long distance, far away from his home in the jungle. In a strange, far away land, devoid of any dark-skinned humans and colder than he had ever experienced, Da-ra was sold to a circus where he had been chained at the ankle and beaten with a whip. It was at the circus that they had taken away his name and given a new one, Siam, one that the humans could pronounce. After the circus, he was sold to the zoo in Munich. Although the zoo was much larger than the circus, where he had been chained at the ankle, it still did not afford him the space necessary to indulge in the kind of exercise he had gotten in the wild. Most of all, Siam wanted to roam again, outside the confines of chains, fences and human interference. Nevertheless, he did as he was told, not wanting to be beaten, knowing all too well that his captors would beat him on the trunk, his most sensitive area, and thus force him to comply with their wishes.

It was at the Munich zoo that he had met the proud Boy, the dominate male and the kindly Cora, who became a surrogate mother to him. Although Siam had considered Boy to be a bit of a braggart, telling anyone who was willing to listen to the long-winded stories of his great warrior lineage, he respected the older male and did his best to keep out of his way. Not yet an adult, Siam was quartered with the females for his safety. Each night, surrounded by Cora, Mini, Toni the Third and the other females, all with new human names, he would go to sleep listening to the story of the elephant goddess, Ha, and the story of how she gave birth to the world, starting with the elephants. Pure white with fiery red eyes, Ha each night turned into the bright silver disc floating in the night sky. If he looked closely, Cora told Siam, he could see her eyes watching down on him. Siam, of course, remembered these stories from his mother, though he couldn't help but wonder why the elephant goddess would allow them all to be in cages or why she allowed his mother to be killed.

Was it possible that Phi-ra, who obviously hated elephants from the beginning, was to blame? And, if Phi-ra was to blame for all of their problems, why did the humans display his cross symbol so proudly? Siam kept these questions to himself not wanting to upset Cora, but hoped that he would one day learn the answers to his questions.

A year after Siam's arrival at the zoo, and a few days after Toni the Third had been taken away to another zoo, Cora gave birth to Boy's first son, Wastl. Siam watched with anticipation as the females helped the new arrival stand in order to be able to reach his mother's milk. Otherwise, Siam knew that the baby would die, and remembered clearly the day of his own birth. He was overjoyed, feeling almost as though he had been granted a little brother and, as Wastl grew stronger, the two young elephants played together in the yard in front of their shelter, kicking around the rubber ball that they had been given. Unfortunately, their friendship was short-lived. When the humans came to take Siam away, just as they had Toni the Third, Wastl screamed his disapproval from behind the bars of his cage, protected by Cora, who wrapped her trunk protectively around her son's head. She would have intervened, but what was the use? The men would have only punished her with whips and the metal rod, the *ankus*, and so she stood beside her baby, silently taking in the scene, tears flowing down her wrinkled face. She let out an anguished groan as she held Wastl to her side, her one act of defiance. Siam dejectedly obeyed his captors, answering his surrogate family with a single, low roar as a goodbye before being prodded up a ramp and into the crate on the back of an already idling lorry. Men jumped onto the back of the lorry and nailed the crate shut, the thundering of their hammers deafening to the young bull. Straps were attached to the crate, anchoring it to the back of the lorry and then all was silent as it lurched away from the zoo and his friends.

***

Siam travelled for five days, first by train from the zoo in Munich and then to the back of a different the lorry, which was driven by a man with a wooly moustache. From there he was transported him to his new home at the zoo in the Tiergarten. Not that he knew any of this. All he knew was that the box was too cramped, that he had been separated from the other elephants and moved a second time since his capture. Siam pulled his face away from the side of the box and sighed heavily, wondering where they were taking him, deciding that anywhere must be better than the inside of his cramped and hot crate. As the lorry rounded a bend in the road and slowed down, Siam pricked up his ears at a familiar sound, his heart racing. When he heard the sound again, the unmistakable cry of a tropical bird, he knew that he wasn't imagining things. He pressed his eye back to the small opening in the crate for another look just as the lorry passed a massive gate, supported at its base by two stone elephants ritually attired in the custom of his homeland. To Siam, the elephants looked as he imagined the elephant goddess, Ha, must look and this comforted him somewhat. Surely, he thought, this is a good sign. Above the gate was a shiny tiled roof, constructed to resemble a pagoda, and below the roof hung a sign bearing the words *"Zoologische Garten."* Though he couldn't understand the lettering, seeing them as only a mass of indiscernible shapes, vastly different from the elephant alphabet, he had the urge to reach out and touch the sign with the tip of his trunk, something that was impossible since he was still confined to the crate and too far away, anyway. Instead, he absently traced the letters on the wall of the crate using his trunk and doing his best to copy the shapes he was seeing. Although an elephant alphabet exists, none of their writings are preserved, often only written in the dirt to teach lessons to the young and gone with the wind and rain. It is for this reason that the story of the goddess and all other lessons passed down from elephant to elephant are primarily an oral tradition.

As the lorry continued along the boulevard a huge building on the opposite side cast a shadow across the crate and, peering out the other side of it, Siam saw a massive stone building, whose top consisted of what appeared to be seven mountains constructed of shiny tiles. Huge openings in the walls appeared to be filled with what looked like colored rocks, but the sun shone through them here and there. This, Siam decided, must have been a temple to the elephant goddess that he had just seen at the gate. He was distracted by the sights around him and nearly lost his footing as the lorry entered a wide square and made a sudden, sharp right turn onto another street. Shifting his weight once again, he could see another large building to his right, this one with a clear top and with shiny yellow metal carriages filled with people going in and out. The carriages even moved above him on raised platforms and rang bells as they moved. Siam had never seen so many people in his life, even at the zoo in Munich, and he realized that he must be in a very important place, a thought that filled him once again with fear. Why, he wondered, would such a young elephant like him be taken to such a big important place? And what would be expected of him? Siam was so lost in his thoughts that he almost failed to notice that the lorry had stopped and turned off its engine. He rushed to press his eye back to the opening in the crate but could only see that the lorry had backed up to a high wall of some sort. Trees stood in the distance, hundreds and hundreds of them, their delicious green canopies taunting him in his cramped box. Siam hoped that this was where they were taking him. It only made sense, after all, that an elephant should live among the trees. Siam suddenly felt lonely and wished that Cora and Wastl could be there with him. Voices from somewhere behind the lorry made Siam lean to the other side of the crate so that he could peer out of the other hole and he could see the driver, the man with the bushy mustache, standing to one side and smoking one of his smelly rolled up papers. He couldn't see who the driver was talking to, as this person was obscured by the crate, but something he said caused the driver to laugh, and he expelled a mouthful of acrid smoke which irritated Siam's nose. Suddenly, there was a commotion somewhere at the back of the lorry and Siam saw the driver hurriedly drop his burning paper and grind it under his foot before removing his hat and straightening his messy hair. The man who had been obscured came into view, moving alongside the driver, no doubt to make way for the new arrival, and his face was as solemn as that of the driver's. Both men bowed slightly, and clicked their heels together and Siam wondered what king he was about to meet. The lorry bounced a little as one of the men jumped onto the back of it and a face appeared at the opening in the crate, peering in. The man, obviously the new arrival, didn't, in Siam's opinion, appear to be a king as he would have imagined a king to appear but instead bore a striking resemblance to the director of the Munich zoo. He had blue eyes and a sharp nose and wore a long, white coat over his clothing. For a moment, Siam wondered if it wasn't the leader from the Munich zoo, there to welcome him to his new home. The human smiled and spoke a few soothing words to Siam before abruptly turning away and barking orders to the men waiting below. Siam heard the loud clang of metal and the hustle of boots on cement. His crate started to sway as a crowbar wielded by an unseen hand began wrenching the nails loose from his enclosure. With an ear-shattering creak the end of the crate was pulled free and light flooded inside, momentarily blinding Siam. As he blinked at the brightness, his heart racing, loud bangs began echoing from the front of the crate accompanied with shouts from the people who were standing on the lorry. It suddenly occurred to Siam that he was expected to turn around and exit. Dutifully, he complied, executing a slow, rocking three-quarter turn in order to face the other way. All the while the shouting and pounding continued. Once he was facing the open end of the crate and his eyes had adjusted to the bright sunlight, Siam could see that the cement walkway was lined on either side with men awaiting his descent. Their leader, who had peered into the crate, stood at the front of the line, his hands clasped behind his back, and he gestured to the man the driver had met at the gate. This man stepped forward grasping a metal rod in his hands, the one Cora had called an *ankus*, and he used the hooked end of the rod to pull Siam by the trunk, encouraging the elephant down the metal ramp. Siam gingerly emerged, cautiously walking down the ramp and onto solid ground. He followed the man up a walkway toward a large building, built to resemble Indian architecture, just inside the wall. The sounds that he had first heard on the street were louder now and more varied. He heard the scream of both bird and monkey, the bray of horses and, to his right, spied a hippopotamus. The cries of thousands of creatures, many different species, filled the air with a chorus unlike anything human hand or heart or ear could have ever created. To Siam it was like being back home in the jungle. Most exciting, however, was the fact that there were elephants somewhere present. Although he had yet to see them, Siam could smell them and could hear their low rumblings. The man leading him was proceeded by two others, who opened two large metal doors at one end of the large building, and Siam followed the man inside. Awaiting them were still other humans, two males and a female, all wearing the white coat that their leader was wearing. They hurriedly began a physical evaluation of the new arrival, forcing his mouth open to inspect his teeth, shoving something into his anus and roughly checking his eyes. Doing his best to endure these indignities, Siam silently evaluated the room that he was in. Sadly, he realized that an elephant had recently died in this room, a male and much older. Siam could smell it, could sense it. Was this another place of eternal sleep? Was this why he had been brought here, he wondered, as a replacement? Before he had time to dwell on these thoughts any longer his quick but thorough inspection was done. Hay and fresh fruits and vegetables were brought in and placed in front of him. The leader appeared in the doorway and spoke with one of the men who had conducted the rough inspection, nodding here and there at what the man was saying and carefully listening as the man read from paper attached to a clipboard. The man with the iron rod appeared in the door next to the leader and, after the elephant inspector was dismissed, the two approached Siam. Siam swayed uneasily from side to side, a habit that he repeated whenever he was nervous. The leader circled the young bull, slapping him triumphantly on the side but without hint of malice. He moved in front of Siam and, as he had done on the lorry, spoke soothingly to him. After a moment's silence, he turned and strode to the door. The man with the iron rod was close at his heels. They exited through the doors, which closed behind them with a clang that echoed in the cavernous space. Siam glanced at the bountiful food heaped before him but was too nervous to eat. The unmistakable scent of death lingered in the room and Siam wondered why he would be put in such a place. He ambled over to the metal door and touched it with his trunk. It was warm from the sun bearing down on it and he pressed his head against the metal only to find that he was most definitely locked in. Siam turned and walked to the other side of the room, whose wall contained a single steel panel. He placed his trunk to this and was certain that there were elephants on the other side of the wall. He looked up at the openings in the wall, but these were set too high in the wall for him to see out. As he stared at the wall in front of him, Siam could make out writing, very faint as if the humans had attempted to scrub it off, but most definitely in elephant script. He turned his head to get a better look at the faint words in front of him, and he shivered when he realized that the words, written in a weak, but defiant style were written in blood.

I AM SI-RA!

Siam backed away from the wall, non-pulsed by the words. Who, he wondered, was Si-ra? Was he the elephant who had died in this room? The thought terrified him, as if the ghost of an elephant was speaking to him.

He turned and walked back to the other side of the room and pressed against the door again, pacing back and forth trying to shake his feelings of dread. With the blood flowing back into his legs and feet, Siam began to relax and realized that he was, indeed, hungry. He walked over to the food that had been left for him and began eating, slowly at first and then with gusto, completely devouring the hay, the melons, the vegetables. A trough under the high windows was filled with water and Siam drank greedily, pulling the water into his trunk and then filling his mouth with the cool liquid. Despite the loneliness he was feeling in his new Spartan quarters, the food and water were good and he could at least move around, a luxury that the crate could not have afforded him. As he prepared himself for sleep later that night, Siam prayed to Ha, thanking her for the food and the water and asked her to protect Cora and Wastl. He also said a prayer for the mysterious Si-ra. If he was, indeed, the elephant who had died in this room Siam wished him a peaceful rest in the place of water.

As he drifted off to sleep, the light from Ha's eye crept in through the high windows and across the concrete floor, eventually finding and gently caressing the sleeping elephant.

Chapter Three

Siam awakened early the next day, after his requisite five hours of sleep, and continued pacing the square, concrete room. Although the courtyard at the Munich zoo had been small, he much more preferred it to these cramped quarters. The weak rays of early sunlight had begun to illuminate the world outside, the sky beyond the high windows a grey-blue color. The elephant script on the wall was still there, confirming that he had not dreamt it up. Siam walked back to the door separating him from the other elephants and placed his trunk to it once again, sniffing the cold steel vigorously. He started at the sudden sound of the double doors opening behind him and turned his head to see the man who had spoken with the leader the day before entering, the metal rod still in his hand. Following him were the three people that had examined Siam, clipboards and equipment in tow. The man with the metal rod stopped in front of Siam and rubbed his rough hands over the elephant's trunk, patting him reassuringly. Siam was grateful for this kindness, much preferring the kind hand over the metal rod with its hook, but this kindness was quickly overshadowed by another rough examination at the hands of the man's three companions. One of them stooped and rudely examined a pile of dung that Siam had earlier deposited on the concrete floor, while the others tugged at his eyes and ears and stuck another instrument in his anus. All the time this was going on the man with the rod continued to massage Siam's trunk, speaking in a low, consoling tone. Although Siam had no idea what he was saying, it was clear to him that his gracious attitude was an attempt to compensate for the rude behavior of the others. Siam knew that, in such small quarters, he could easily kill all four humans but remained patient. As notes were fastidiously jotted down onto a piece of paper attached to a board held by one of the trio, they continued their prodding. After half an hour the trio suddenly ceased their examination to stand in a corner to discuss their findings, speaking in hushed tones. After a moment of this one of the men in the trio called to the man with the rod, who immediately stopped patting Siam's trunk and joined them. After a brief conversation the man with the rod smiled and nodded, turning to look at Siam, his eyes gleaming. Without another word the four disappeared through the door, slamming it shut behind them. Siam looked at the floor, puzzled. Unlike the day before, they had failed to bring hay and fruit and he wondered whether he had done something wrong. Surely, he thought, the fact that he had allowed them to poke and prod him was reason enough to warrant fresh food. He turned back to the steel panel on the opposite wall and was just about to touch it with his trunk when, with a grating screech, it lifted up from the floor powered by an unseen force. He shrunk back in terror, his ears raised, confused by this sudden occurrence, and stood for a couple of minutes staring at the doorway that had magically appeared in the wall. He considered retreating to the other side of the room, but curiosity compelled him to stick his trunk through the opening. The smell of other elephants was too much to bear, so, with beating heart, Siam slowly approached the opening. Ever so slowly he stuck his head through. On the other side of the wall were, indeed, elephants milling about in the courtyard in front of the shelter, among them Toni the Third. Mustering all of the courage he had, Siam propelled himself through the opening, and into a larger room with vaulted ceilings. Sparrows, who had built nests among the rafters of the room, flew out into the courtyard ahead of him.

"*Elephant! Elephant! Elephant!*" they announced.

Siam greeted Toni the Third excitedly, and she smiled widely, just as happy to see her surrogate nephew. The other elephants, two males and a female with her young child turned their heads as one, and slowly gathered around the new arrival. The child, a female called Kalifa the Second, took a couple of steps toward Siam while staying close to her mother, and let out a playful squeal. Siam snorted in response and lumbered out into the opening with the other elephants, his ears raised in anticipation. Another elephant, slightly larger than Siam, approached, mimicking Siam's pose. This elephant introduced himself as Carl, playfully touching Siam's trunk with his own in mock battle. Although he and Siam were the same age, Carl was an African Elephant, so he was slightly larger with larger ears than Siam's, but with much less hair than the smaller Asian Elephant. He pushed his body against the new arrival, slowly emitting a series of low, friendly rumbles. Siam, who had at this point completely forgotten about the lack of food, was overjoyed at being reunited with Toni the Third and in the company of elephants once again. He explained to Carl that he had just arrived the day before from the zoo in Munich where he had known Toni the Third, and Carl explained that he, too, had been brought to Berlin from another zoo, one located in a place called Hannover. Like Siam, he had been born in the wild but had been at the Berlin zoo for nine years. Before that, he had lived in a country called Zimbabwe, where he had been in a clan composed of him, his mother, sisters and aunts. As Carl spoke of his lost clan a sad, wistful expression filled his eyes and Siam expected that their stories were probably similar. Being in such a good mood, however, he decided not to pry. Following elephant protocol, Siam approached the matriarch, Mary, in the submissive posture, ears flattened, back arched and tail raised. He placed the tip of his trunk in her mouth out of respect and she responded by touching the top of his head with her own trunk. Siam impetuously asked about the dead elephant, the one he smelled in the solitary chamber.

"Who was Si-ra?" he blurted.

He immediately felt embarrassed at his gaffe when he saw the expressions on the faces of the other elephants. Mary suddenly dropped her head and groaned and large tears appeared in her sad eyes, while her child, Kalifa the second, let out an anguished cry and leaned against her mother for comfort. The other elephant, a small sixteen year old elephant named Mampe, looked aghast and walked away from the group to the edge of the enclosure, and silently stared out across the zoo grounds. Toni the Third, who had apparently been a bit more tactful upon the occasion of her own arrival, looked away. The dead elephant, Carl sadly explained, had been called Harry by the humans and had suddenly died two months earlier at the age of fifty-three. Fed up with the mundane life of the zoo, he had become aggressive and had killed a human, an elephant keeper. As a result, he had been placed in isolation away from the other elephants. There he had grown mad, screaming over and over his elephant name and refusing to acknowledge the name given him by the humans. Locked away from the other elephants, shamed and broken, he died alone. Carl pointed with his trunk toward the room where Siam had spent his first night, as if to make his point.

As was elephant custom, Carl continued, Harry's surviving clan was still in mourning and were especially saddened because the humans had taken Harry's body away, making it impossible for the elephants to pay regular homage to him, an important elephant tradition. Mary, who was a respectable thirty years old, had been brought straight to the zoo from the wild and had coupled with Harry almost immediately, impressed with the power and charm of the wise, older bull. Since his death she had been almost inconsolable, but did her best to keep her mourning to a minimum if only for the sake of their child, Kalifa the Second. Mampe, on the other hand, made no attempt to hide his grief and stood for hours in Harry's regular spot beside the bare tree, silently groaning and swaying back and forth. Mampe, Carl continued, was a dwarf elephant who, after reaching his current size, had simply stopped growing and had adored the much older and larger Harry, acting almost like a subservient female around him. But being impressed by Harry was easy, explained Carl, as he could enthrall any elephant with his stories of elephant glory, tracing his lineage back to the Mongols, the pharos and Alexander the Great. This reminded Siam of Boy and similar stories, and he silently wondered whether older elephants merely made these stories up to impress the young. Instead of voicing his doubts and risking another affront to his new friends, Siam commented that Harry sounded a lot like Boy, an elephant that he and Toni the Third had known at the Munich zoo. At the mention of Boy's name Mampe suddenly broke his silence, slowly approaching the two younger bulls, his ears perked up. He was happy to hear that Boy was doing well, explaining that he, Boy and Harry had all been at the Hamburg zoo together before Harry, and then later, Mampe had been moved to Berlin. They had assumed all this time, before the arrival of Toni the Third, anyway, that Boy was still in Hamburg. Even the Fog Crows, who arrived in Berlin each November on their migratory pattern from the south, had failed to share this information with them, though admittedly, Mampe still had trouble understanding their gibberish. Siam was relieved to see that mention of Boy had seemingly raised the small elephant's spirits, but Mary remained standing to one side, sadness lingering in her large eyes. He slowly approached the matriarch again, his head low, and she touched the top of his head delicately with the tip of her trunk, forgiving him his accidental faux pas with a series of low rumbles. He was, she reminded herself, still young and apt to make many mistakes before reaching a respectable age. Kalifa the Second, who had already forgotten why she was crying, peeked around her mother's leg and blinked her bright eyes at Siam. He laughed at her shameless flirting and extended his trunk to playfully touch the five year old, and she squealed with delight, retreating to the other side of Mary, where she again peeked at Siam. He turned, happy that all was forgiven, and walked back to the two males. Toni the Third, in turn, rejoined the females. Mampe had resumed talking about the proud Boy and Carl seemed grateful that Siam had returned if only for a change of subject. Siam mentioned the stone elephants flanking the gate he had passed on the wide boulevard, and Mampe, who had been born in the wild, trumpeted loudly at the mention of the gate, his distaste evident. When pressed by Siam, who thought that the gate was constructed out of reverence for the elephant goddess, Mampe snorted loudly.

> "Why do you believe that humans would ever honor the elephant goddess while keeping her children behind bars? The gate," Mampe insisted, "is a bad joke on the part of the humans, who only keep elephants for their own petty amusement."

That said, the dwarf elephant abruptly turned away from the two young males and walked back to the bare tree, where he resumed his brooding silence. Siam, who feared that he had just misspoken a second time since his arrival, moaned apologetically, but Carl motioned him to follow him to a far part of the yard. Siam followed, and walked around the elephant house and they stopped at the far end of the structure. Carl quietly explained to Siam that the subject of the elephant gate was a touchy one, especially for Mampe, who was still angry that his friend, Harry, had been forced to live and die in such a place.

> "Of course," he went on, "we have all seen the gate and initially assumed, like you, that it was some sort of human tribute to the goddess."

And, after all, the gate was in a prominent place making just such an assumption easy to reach.

> "But," Carl was quick to point out, "there is another gate, this one decorated with lions, and the lions are in no better condition than we elephants, so

how can the elephant gate be any more or less than what Mampe suggested it is?"

Siam's initial joy at seeing the gate was instantly gone and he wanted to argue that it must have meant something good for the elephants, but Carl had already turned and was walking back towards the group. Sensing Siam's confusion, he explained that it was feeding time, and Siam hurried to catch up, noticing upon rounding the building that the elephants were all dutifully entering the building at the behest of the man with the iron rod. The man smiled and spoke softly to each animal as it passed him and seemed to show special interest in Siam as he mimicked the others. Once inside, standing behind the bars and beneath the vaulted ceiling, a group of men entered the yard and began dumping sweet-smelling hay onto the ground. On top of that they placed fruits and vegetables, more food than Siam had ever seen at one time, even at the Munich zoo and certainly more than at the circus. When the workers were done and had left the yard, the man with the iron rod opened the gate and the elephants ambled toward the food, Mary first followed by Kalifa and then Toni the Third, Mampe and Carl. Siam was the last to enter the yard, not wanting to step out of line again on his first day. As they ate, he told Carl that he had never seen so much food and Carl, who was busy eating a melon, its orange pulp splattered on the ground, merely grunted, replying that the zoo was enormous, with thousands and thousands of animals of every breed possible. He honestly didn't know how many creatures lived behind the bars of the zoo but, he added, munching on hay, there were far more animals than the biggest elephant clan even in the best of times. It was this knowledge that initially filled the elephants with trepidation, for even elephants had the wisdom to divide into separate clans with distinct territories, and so many animals in one place had raised doubts about the possibility of food shortages. After so many feedings, however, their fears had slowly dissipated, as they realized that, under such controlled circumstances, there was little possibility of shortage or famine. The general consensus was that only an incredible act of stupidity on the part of their captors would ever lead to food shortages. Siam looked away from Carl and noticed that the leader of the zoo had approached and was, alongside the man with the iron rod, watching the elephants from outside their enclosure, separated by a wide, deep moat. He commented to Carl that the leader greatly resembled the leader of the Munich zoo. Mampe, having overheard, snorted loudly. He explained that the leader of the Berlin and Munich zoos were brothers, a little tidbit he had learned from the migrating crows. Quickly digesting this new information, Siam turned back to the zoo leader, wondering how it was possible that one family could produce two sons that would imprison animals, a question he repeated to Mampe, who snorted loudly again. He explained that the Berlin zoo leader had taken over the job from his father only two years earlier. Siam looked to Carl to make sure Mampe wasn't making the story up, but Carl was busy eating hay, obviously unimpressed with the conversation. Instead, it was Mary who piped up, commenting that, while she didn't understand their captivity, she truly believed that the humans meant well. How else could their ample food be explained? And besides, she added, not unkindly, young Kalifa was far safer having been born at the zoo than in the wild. Here at least, she added, making her point, the lions and hyenas were kept well away from the elephant young. Perhaps, she concluded, it was the goddess' plan to keep them safe, even if they were unable to understand. Besides, she added, the zoo director seemed more interested in breeding prehistoric cows than in harming elephants. She stared at Mampe pointedly for a moment before resuming her feeding. As Mary spoke, Kalifa regarded her mother in silence. Siam dared not contradict the matriarch and turned back to the zoo leader, who had disappeared along with the man with the iron rod.

***

That afternoon, seemingly recovered from his depression, Mampe joined Siam at the edge of the moat. He proudly pointed out the various buildings that surrounded them. Despite his protestations to the contrary, the little African Elephant spoke almost affectionately of the zoo, pointing out the three-story aquarium in the distance, the ostrich house, which had been built in Egyptian style, and the antelope house. Flamingos, a moving sea of pink, moved silently in their enclosure just to the right of them and somewhere nearby a large cat growled. The light above was bright and, as Mampe wandered back to his tree, Siam tossed dirt onto his back and flapped his ears to cool off. Mary and Kalifa stood near the elephant house, silently swaying in the bright light, while Carl raised his trunk and his large ears in the direction of a group of people who had gathered to stare at them from the other side of the moat. Regarding a light-haired woman in a very bright, red dress, Siam thought that, perhaps Mary was right, perhaps this was what the goddess had planned for them. And, if the humans truly meant well as Mary had suggested, perhaps Mampe was wrong about the elephant gate, as well. This thought alone made Siam smile, and he trumpeted loudly at the humans on the other side of the moat, despite himself.

Chapter Four

Two months had passed since his arrival at the Berlin zoo, and Siam had formed a close bond with Carl, who was slowly introducing him to their surroundings, the two spending long hours together in the courtyard watching the throngs of passing humans, all pale-skinned and most with hair the color of dried grass, although others had dark hair. For Siam, Carl's friendship helped fill the void left by his sudden separation from Wastl, and he had quickly been accepted by the other elephants, under the watchful eye of Mary, the matriarch, as part of their zoo clan. Although life in the zoo was somewhat tedious, Siam had grown accustomed to the regular feedings and even the excellent medical care, even if he didn't care for the rough handling at the hands of the staff. And, as in Munich, he longed for more space in which to roam and was jealous of the sparrows, which nested in the rafters and could come and go from the zoo as they wished.

Siam was becoming acquainted with the other animals in the zoo, as well. Although separated by cages, moats, sandpits and even buildings, the cries and howls of the other animals carried news to the elephant house, news regarding new arrivals, births and deaths. The parrots, in particular, were a good source for gossip, just as they had been in the jungles. While each animal possessed its own language particular to its species, there is, in the animal kingdom, a simple language that conveys, even intra-species, the most basic news that might prove useful elsewhere. It was via this language that Siam first met Rosa, the hippopotamus, Arra, a seventy-five year old parrot, Roland the Sea Lion and a gorilla named Bobby. Bobby, Mampe commented with what almost seemed like a hint of jealousy, was a bit of a star at the zoo, his photograph gracing the covers of the zoo guides given to visitors. Mampe grimaced at the sparrows as they broke into a chorus.

"Bobby! Bobby! Bobby!"

Mary quietly interjected that Harry, too, had been photographed for the cover of the zoo guide and, in fact, many animals at the zoo had shared that honor. Siam silently wondered if Mampe's jealousy stemmed from the fact that he would have liked his own image on the cover of the zoo guide, but refrained from asking, not wanting to offend the older male, who was still in a deep depression over the death of Harry. An outdoor café near the massive aquarium building played music over its loudspeakers and this seemed to be the only thing that Mampe enjoyed, and he would stand for hours beside the bare tree, silently swaying to the tunes that drifted through the fall air. Aside from this one diversion, Mampe had withdrawn even more, rarely speaking with the other elephants and only speaking when he had something critical to say about the zoo or another animal at the zoo, or to speak of Africa and the day he would return there. He had even begun to eat less, a development that prompted harsh words from the otherwise docile Mary, who warned him that he would get sick if he didn't eat, especially with the winter approaching. Stubbornly, however, he ignored her admonishments. Realizing that this behavior was not unusual for a bull of sixteen who, in the wild, would have already left the company of females to join an all-male bachelor herd, Mary allowed this small act of rebellion to pass without incident. Siam listened to Mampe's plans of his return to Africa and wondered just how the morose little elephant hoped to accomplish such a feat. Siam, too, missed his homeland and didn't relish another cold winter in a strange land so, if Mampe truly had a plan to leave the zoo, then Siam would join him. He told Carl this, but Carl merely snorted and shook his head, commenting that the older bull was going crazy and that there was no way he would ever go back to Africa. Mary, too, secretly worried that Mampe's condition was dire and, using her matriarchal authority, silently implored Siam and Carl to rally to the older bull's side in the elephant custom of never abandoning a fallen comrade. They did their best, despite Mampe's sour attitude, and each day endeavored to involve him in their play and conversations, even leaving the best bits of fruit for him during feedings. He usually ignored their offerings, instead allowing the sparrows to pick at the food on the ground. This, of course, filled Siam with a deep sadness for the mourning elephant, and each night he silently asked the goddess to help Mampe out of his depression. As for himself, Siam was being plagued by visions of his own homeland, and each night was visited in dreams by his mother, who was painted from head to toe by the hooked crosses he had seen on the red and white banners in Munich and Berlin. One afternoon, after a particularly fitful night's sleep during which Carl nearly pushed his fidgety friend from the elephant house for keeping everyone else awake, Siam mentioned the symbol to Carl. Carl looked up at one of the banners, which was affixed to a pole just outside their enclosure, and was about to speak when Mampe interrupted. Although Carl was slightly offended by the interruption he held his tongue, a quick glance from Mary reminding him that keeping Mampe involved in conversation was good. Kalifa the Second stopped chasing a large black and yellow butterfly and giggled at Carl, who sheepishly wagged his ears in response. Mary wrapped her trunk around Kalifa the Second in an attempt to save Carl's wounded pride, and the baby quickly forgot what she was doing and resumed chasing the butterfly. Mampe, who seemed oblivious to the elaborate charade taking place around him, looked up at the banner fluttering from its pole and pointed at it with his trunk, and explained to Siam that the banners were a relatively new thing.

> "At first," he continued, "they had only been seen here and there, sometimes only worn on the arms of some of the humans but, early in the year when it was still very cold, they had suddenly multiplied, appearing on every pole visible."

As far as the elephants could discern, the symbol belonged to a new ruling class among the humans and, suddenly, more and more humans had begun wearing them on their arms. Mary and Toni the Third, Asian elephants like Siam, shared the young bull's memory of the symbol and didn't believe that it could be anything bad, despite its association with Phi-ra. In typical fashion, however, Mampe shook his head in disagreement, commenting that there was something ominous about the showy red, white and black banners and, in his opinion, such behavior on the part of the humans would only lead to bad things. Mary raised her head ominously, despite her insistence for leniency toward the ailing bull.

"How can an African elephant understand the symbols of my homeland?" she asked.

Toni the Third loudly agreed. Carl, the other African elephant was, for once, inclined to agree with Mampe but kept silent out of respect for the matriarch. Embarrassed by her quick reaction, Mary quickly softened, offering to Mampe the suggestion that he might be right, that one could only wait and see how things developed. With humans, she added sarcastically, things always seemed to change so quickly. Mampe nodded, a tired expression on his face, and slowly ambled back to his tree, where he stood and gazed across the lake where the flamingoes stood lazily in the November sun. Four sparrows, who had been silently watching the exchange, flew up and landed on his back. Carl, Siam, Toni the Third and Mary all exchanged silent glances, conveying without words that they had at least tried. Carl walked around to the far side of the elephant house in search of any over-reaching branches that might still bear any edible leaves and Mary turned her attentions to her daughter, joined by Toni the Third.

Siam turned around and looked across the moat, where he saw a human staring intently at him. The man smiled at the young elephant. Obviously an older human because of the long, white beard that cascaded from his chin like a waterfall and the wiry white hairs that protruded from beneath his hat, he seemed somehow melancholy to Siam, despite the kindness in his eyes. Siam raised his ears and trunk in reply, eliciting a bigger smile from the old man, who feebly waved a pale hand at the young bull. Emboldened by the attention, Siam raised a leg as he had been taught at the circus in Munich and trumpeted a greeting to the human. The old man laughed and nodded his head and looked back at the young elephant many times as he walked away from the elephant enclosure. Once the old man was completely out of sight, Siam said to Mary that the old man was perhaps the first human that he had not disliked. Mary touched the top of the young elephant's head with her trunk and replied that it was her belief that not all humans were bad, something that he and Carl would do well to remember. Siam took this gentle criticism gracefully, for he had truly begun to admire the wise and patient matriarch.

To his surprise, the old man re-appeared the next day at the exact same time. At first Siam had not noticed the old man standing patiently to the side, but Mary did, and nudged the young bull awake from his nap. Siam walked to the edge of the deep moat and repeated his act of flapping his ears and waving his trunk at the visitor, which again brought a smile to his lined old face. The old man clapped his hands gleefully as Siam once again raised his leg and trumpeted a hearty blast in his direction. With shaky hands the old man produced from a pocket on his overcoat a small, white bag, which was twisted closed at one end. Carefully, he produced a peanut, which he held toward Siam in offering. Siam extended his trunk as far as he could without toppling into the moat but couldn't reach the small gift. After peering side to side to make sure that there were no witnesses to his petty crime, the old man tossed the peanut over the moat and into the elephant enclosure. Siam took a moment to locate the tiny legume but, using the single fingertip at the end of his trunk to gingerly lift it from the ground. He placed the gift in his mouth, relishing the feel of the patterned shell on his tongue and crushed it with his molars. Siam had never tasted a peanut before, even during his time in Munich, but the disappointing size of the tiny nut made him instantly want more. He once again held his trunk out expectantly and the old man repeated his secret feeding, this time tossing two peanuts in front of the elephant. One landed precariously close to the edge of the moat but Siam quickly gathered it up and, to the delight of the old man, devoured both. Before Siam could request more peanuts he was surprised to see a shower of peanuts landing in front of him, and looked up to see the old man quietly stuffing the empty paper bag back into his pocket. Siam dejectedly noted that a few stray peanuts had landed at the bottom of the moat, well out of his reach, but began gathering up the bounty at his feet before the sparrows could snatch any. The old man was happily watching the elephant devour his gift when loud voices on the walkway broke the spell, causing them both to look in the direction of the noise. Approaching the elephant enclosure were two men dressed in brown from head to toe and wearing boots similar to those of the circus keepers in Munich. On their arms were the red and white banners with the black cross in the middle, and the old man fled as quickly as his feet would carry him in the direction of the bird house. The new arrivals continued shouting after him, rudely, and then broke into raucous laughter, not unlike the sound of parrots in the tree canopy. Siam looked to make sure the old man had gotten safely away and then turned to regard the new arrivals, both fairly young in human years. They were now staring at Siam and he wondered whether he was in trouble for taking the peanuts. But, when he didn't do anything, the two moved on, obviously disinterested in

Siam or any of the other elephants. Siam turned to Mary and asked her why the two men had chased off the older human. She stood, regarding the young bull with a deep sadness in her eyes but, before she could reply, Mampe's voice came drifting to him from beneath the tree.

> "The new ruling class," he explained, his voice flat and humorless, "apparently doesn't like certain humans and that old human is one of them."

Confused, Siam turned back to where the old man had been standing and sniffed the air. He didn't smell any differently than any of the other humans that Siam had encountered, and the only obvious difference was his beard, facts that Siam pointed out to Mampe. This time it was Mary who spoke, her voice tired.

> "It was the way of humans," she pointed out, "to be in-human."

"Inhuman! Inhuman! Inhuman!" shouted the sparrows.

How else could Siam explain his mother's death? But, Mary added, as she often said, humans never stick to anything too long, so it was her hope that it would all pass quickly. Siam silently digested this new information and walked back to the edge of the moat, where the only remaining peanuts rested at the bottom. Already, a mouse was there dragging one off to its nest. He regarded a couple of humans, a man and a woman walking past the enclosure and wondered whether they, like the old man, were disliked by the new ruling class. He again sniffed the air after them but could discern no difference between them and the old man or even the two men in boots.

***

That night, after the elephants had been herded into the elephant house and had drifted off to sleep, Siam and Carl were awakened by frenzied screams from Mary and Toni the Third. As the two young bulls shook themselves awake and their eyes adjusted to the semi-darkness, they saw that Mampe was lying on the cold concrete floor and breathing erratically. The sparrows, awakened by the tumult, peered down from their nests in the rafters. Prodded by instructions from Mary, the two bulls were able to pull the dwarf elephant to his feet and keep him standing by placing their bodies on either side of his small frame. Mary ran to the bars that separated them from the yard and frantically called for the humans, her cries echoing across the darkened zoo grounds. Each time she screamed, Kalifa the Second let out a tiny squeal, tears standing in her eyes. Although Mary knew that the humans would not understand her cries, she knew that the other animals would understand her distress and, hopefully, relay word to the humans. Rosa, the hippopotamus, roared in response and slowly, word passed across the landscape. Apes and birds screamed, horses brayed and wolves howled and, after twenty minutes, the man with the iron rod appeared, clearly angry at having been awakened. Upon inspecting the scene, however, he exited the elephant house and quickly reappeared with two of the humans that had twice examined Siam upon his arrival. They, too, looked tired and a bit irritated, but moved quickly into the elephant's quarters carrying their equipment. The man with the iron rod started roughly pushing at Siam in order to move him away from Mampe, but Siam's initial reaction was to remain where he was standing. He was seconds from pushing the human to the floor when Mary screamed over the tumult that Siam needed to move so that the humans could help. Siam instantly moved to one side, allowing the humans access and Carl followed suit. Incredibly, the dwarf remained standing, though his eyes indicated that he was quickly leaving them. The man with the iron rod herded the two young bulls into the separate pen with Toni the Third, Mary and Kalifa the Second. The five elephants pressed their faces to the bars, their trunks reaching toward the sick elephant, intently watching the activity on the other side. The man with the iron rod stood to one side, shaking his head and muttering under his breath and, when Mampe again collapsed to the concrete floor, Mary pushed Kalifa the Second away from the bars so that she couldn't see. The humans continued frantically working on the felled bull, but when Mampe expelled one last muffled groan, Siam turned his wet face away, unable to look.

Was it the name of the goddess, Ha, he had muttered at the end? Or was he still looking for his old friend Harry?

Chapter Five

1934

Following the death of Mampe the elephant herd conducted the ritual of mourning, a task made more difficult for Toni the Third, Mary, Kalifa the Second and Carl, mere months after the death of Harry. Siam felt doubly bad for the others, having lost two of their own in such a short period of time, and he joined them in their mourning process over the little dwarf elephant, each day visiting his bare tree in the middle of the yard to pay homage to him. It was only the fact that Mampe was indeed free of the zoo as he had wished that bolstered Siam's spirits. This was the sole concession he was willing to allow his captors, in fact viewing Mampe's death as an escape of sorts. Besides, he thought, maybe Mampe had returned to Africa, after all. Nobody knew or truly understood the mysteries of the goddess and perhaps this had been the only way he could truly leave the zoo in the end. But that concession was all that Siam was willing to offer. Having had to endure the spectacle of the removal of Mampe's lifeless body from the shelter had been difficult to bear, especially for Kalifa the Second, whose piercing cries had nearly drowned out the sound of the lorry that carted the carcass away after the humans had lifted it from the floor using a specially designed apparatus that they attached to the ceiling of the shelter. Even Carl, who whispered to Siam that the elephant house would be a bit more pleasant without Mampe's constant complaining, had roared at the humans as they callously manipulated the little elephant's body, dangling it above the lorry before uncermoniously dropping it onto the idling machine's bed. The sparrows, too, high in the rafters, seemed offended and fluttered above the scene in frenzy. Despite Carl's apparent ambivalence over Mampe's death only two months after the fact, outside of the traditional elephant mourning, Siam suspected that it had affected him far more deeply than he admitted. For instance, the familiar music, which drifted from the nearby pavilion and which Carl had never before shown any opinion of, now seemed to make him angry and he would trumpet loudly, as if trying to drown it out. This, Siam suspected, was because it reminded Carl of Mampe, although he didn't share this theory with anyone, afraid of offending Carl. In fact, within days of Mampe's death, Siam could detect a transformation taking place in his new friend, one that he had first recognized as mourning but, as the weeks passed, realized that it was something more. Mary, who was doing her best to remain the strong matriarch, caring first for her child, Kalifa the Second, and second for her two surrogate sons, Carl and Siam, quietly explained to Siam that Carl was maturing and that, with the death of Mampe, was now the dominant bull. Siam silently accepted this explanation but, since he had no interest in being the dominant bull, couldn't understand why this new development would change his friend's demeanor. Mary laughed softly and closed her eyes, finding Siam's trunk and entwining it with her own. She whispered that the time was soon coming when he would understand and she hoped that Siam would remember his place within the herd when that time arrived. Siam appreciated Mary's words, but still found it difficult to understand the importance of who was dominant and who was not. Mary, of course, was the matriarch, this he could accept, and if Carl, the larger, African elephant, chose to be the dominant male, who was Siam to argue? Mary laughed softly again. "Remember that when the time comes," she said.

Siam assured her that he would and Mary turned her attention to Kalifa the Second, who was playing with Toni the Third.

Fortunately, a welcome diversion arrived in November in the form of the migrating Fog Crows. Although Siam was instantly fascinated with the loud black and white birds, their fluttering forms darkening the skies over the zoo as they headed to roosting grounds in the nearby Tiergarten, the sparrows seemed offended by their presence.

"*Go away! Go away! Go away!*"

The crows ignored the sparrows and noisily shouted news from above regarding the weather and other animals, though Siam had difficulty understanding their crow gibberish, much as Mampe had described. Hesitantly, Siam asked Carl if they had reported any news from Munich. Carl acted as if Siam had interrupted something important, although he was merely standing by the tree as usual, and he snorted loudly at Siam that it was up to him to learn the crow's dialect on his own. Mary quickly stepped between the two males, first reminding Carl that it was she and Harry who had helped him to learn the dialect, and then she turned to Siam and spoke with an apologetic, motherly air.

> "No," she patiently explained, "I heard no mention of Munich, but the crows will be back. They often remain in the city for a few days before continuing their migration east."

This reassurance relieved Siam, who only longed for some news of his surrogate family in Munich, and he quickly excused Carl's harsh words. The next day, Siam was rewarded for his patience with the appearance of two of the crows during first feeding. Black with white heads, the crows had at first landed on top of the elephant house but, seeing the food scraps on the ground among the elephants, quickly descended and picked through the small morsels that the elephants ignored. Offended that their food had been stolen, the sparrows took flight, landing on Siam's back. The crows, both males, who hurriedly introduced themselves as Yach and Blach, bickered at each other and fought over the available scraps. Excited by their noisy arrival, Siam quickly forgot his appetite and approached the crow named Yach, extending his trunk in greeting. The crow seemed offended by the prodding trunk and hopped quickly out of the path of the lumbering elephant. Unwilling to be deterred, Siam persisted, provoking a harsh retort from the old bird. His friend, Blach, laughed heartily, informing Yach in crow gibberish that the elephant only wanted to say hello. Yach, however, seemed to be in a bad mood. When Blach explained that he was still angry because a human had shot at them in a field near Munich, Siam's ears perked up.

"What news of the Munich zoo?" he blurted.

"Were the elephants there well? Had they all weathered the season well?"

His questions came so quickly that both crows squawked at him in unison. Silenced by their rebuff, Siam backed away, an expectant look on his face. The two visitors thought for a moment, then blurted out all they could remember from the Munich zoo, twice contradicting each other which led to a vigorous argument. Siam impatiently interrupted their argument by exhaling air onto the ground in front of them. They both looked very insulted, but continued their story, explaining that all of the elephants there had seemed well with the exception of the older female, Cora, who was very pregnant. Siam was overjoyed by this news and, since they had mentioned

Cora by name, knew that they were telling the truth. He trumpeted a thank you to the crows and shared the news with Toni the Third, who seemed happy to hear news of her old friends. Mary, who had at that point finished eating, smiled at Siam, happy that he had received the news he had hoped to receive. She tenderly twined her trunk with his.

> "See," she said, "the goddess is bringing blessings just as she had said and, following her lead, Cora is bringing a new life into the world, just as the trees are now losing their leaves."

Siam contemplated the words of the wise matriarch but, before he could reply, the crows noisily departed, taking flight and heading in the direction of the Tiergarten.

***

Siam silently regarded Carl, who was standing in the yard alone, snow lightly falling from the gray sky above and gathering on his back like thousands of massed white flies. The winter, only in its first quarter, was bitterly cold and the humans in their white coats and rubber boots did everything they could to make the elephants comfortable, taking special care to tend to the elephant's skin, which became sore and brittle in the cold, stinging wind. Wrapped in their clothing, which they pulled tightly around their necks, the humans didn't appear to like the cold weather any more than the elephants, and Siam wondered why any creature would choose to live in such conditions. Nevertheless, the humans continued to bring food and to offer medical care so Siam endeavored to make it through as best as he could, although all he could think about was the day when it would be warm again. Kalifa the Second, on the other hand, seemed to relish the cold weather, and tossed snowballs at Siam, Toni the Third and Carl. Once, over the protests of her mother, she tossed a snowball at a zoo visitor, although these humans were rare in the cold weather. In response, Carl had growled at Kalifa the Second but, aware of his place under Mary, had left his protest at a single growl. In turn, Mary half-heartedly admonished her daughter but then suggested to Carl that he might try to enjoy the snow since they were stuck with it for another three months. Carl only snorted an unintelligible reply before turning away and Mary offered a knowing wink to Siam. Siam smiled at the matriarch's playful attitude but couldn't help but sympathize with Carl, understanding all too well the unnatural position they were all in. Elephants didn't belong in these cold conditions, none that Siam had ever met, anyway, and so Carl's grumpiness was not completely unfounded. This, and the fact that he must have been feeling a great deal of pressure at suddenly having been thrust into the role of dominant male, made Siam respect his friend even more.

***

As the winter progressed over the following months, it only seemed to get colder and the unwelcome snow piled up in drifts outside the animal houses faster than the humans could remove it. The tropical birds seemed to be the unhappiest of the creatures among the zoo's menagerie and, each night, Siam would listen to them curse the bitter cold, pining for such places as Madagascar, Cameroon and Bolivia. Even the goddess seemed to have deserted them, her image barely discernable in the cloudy, snow-filled skies. But Mary quietly reminded Siam that, in winter, the goddess merely rested and all else followed suit out of respect. How else could the slumber of the earth in this cold place be explained? And, with the reawakening of the goddess in the spring, all else would once again reawaken, bringing back food and bright light. Even in the wild, elephants followed this pattern, in the rainy season finding food on the ground and in the dry season eating from the trees. This, Mary concluded, was the eternal story and, as elephants, they must never forget, for memory was an elephant's greatest asset followed only by loyalty. These were the gifts of the goddess.

Siam wondered whether Boy, Cora, Wastl and the other elephants in Munich were as miserable and wished the crows would bring news of them. At the mention of the crows, Carl laughed, suddenly snapped from his dark mood. Where Mampe had always seemed to have been irritated by the foreign chatter of the winged visitors, Carl truly enjoyed the diversion they brought with them on their visits and explained to Siam that they would not arrive again until the next fall. Siam sighed, picturing the bare surrounding trees once again filled with leaves, leaves that offered both shade and sustenance. Siam commented that he hoped the cold would be short-lived, eliciting a sharp retort from Carl, who echoed Mary's earlier admonition about enjoying the weather while it lasted. Stung from what he felt was an unfair attack, Siam turned away from Carl and walked around the elephant house where he found Kalifa the Second making florid designs in the snow with her trunk. He quietly watched her for a moment before interrupting, praising her for her beautiful creations, depictions of lush trees, flowers and butterflies. Kalifa the Second blushed and regarded the older bull with a twinkle in her eye. Without saying another word Siam moved beside her and, in a patch of unblemished snow, began drawing his own creation, a rough likeness of the man with the iron rod, which caused Kalifa the Second to squeal with delight. Playfully, she tossed a scoop of snow, which hit Siam in the middle of his forehead, before hurrying back to the safety of her mother and Toni the Third. Siam laughed and shook the snow from his head. He gave a half-hearted, playful chase, which caused the young female to squeal louder. Mary, who Kalifa the Second had taken refuge behind, playfully scolded them with a low growl, but they knew from her posture that she wasn't serious. Carl stood silently to the side, unwilling to join in no matter how much Siam tried to engage him.

Carl's air of detachment continued over the course of the following months and he had become so engrossed in his new role of dominant male that Siam and Kalifa the Second formed their own special bond. If Carl wanted to play the part of the serious adult then that was fine with Siam. He was more than happy to relinquish that role and to play with Kalifa the Second, instead. For Siam, Kalifa the

Second's childishness was a welcome diversion from the daily drudgery of the zoo and she made him feel alive, much as the baby, Wastl, had in Munich. As for Mary, while she appreciated how happy her daughter was, she was worried by this new friendship, knowing that Siam would soon begin to reach maturity. Since Kalifa the Second would not reach maturity for another four to eight summers, she worried what might happen between them. Not that she mistrusted the young bull, anymore than she mistrusted Carl, but male urges were difficult to control, this much she had learned in her own twenty summers. Instead of worrying about the matter, however, Mary decided it best to patiently wait and watch. The goddess would show her what to do when the time came, this she trusted.

***

By the time the snow began to melt and the first buds began appearing on the trees, Mary's suspicions were confirmed when she noticed a change in Siam's demeanor. Still not quite ready for mating, Siam was beginning to show the first rebellious signs of bull adulthood. Kalifa the Second seemed largely oblivious to the change, an oversight for which Mary was grateful, not wanting her daughter's feelings to be hurt. Unfortunately, however, Siam and Carl had begun sparring as adolescent bulls are apt to do, and Mary had to step in on occasion in the role of matriarch to restore peace to the elephant house. These disagreements, of course, had mostly to do with the sudden attention Carl had begun to pay Toni the Third and Kalifa the Second, a new development which filled Siam with jealousy. Where Toni the Third was unequivocally opposed to mating with the young bull, Kalifa the Second was completely oblivious to the real meaning of Carl's advances.

With the first signs of spring appearing around him, crocus popping up in the sandy soil, buds appearing on the trees, and the return of the migrating birds, Siam, too, felt as if he was awakening from a slumber. The days were slowly growing longer and, though there was still a chill in the air, the biting cold of winter was fading. He looked up at the sounds of geese, flying overhead and headed north. It was a reassuring sound, one that meant warm weather was retuning, and Siam smiled.

When they had vanished from sight, Siam looked back down and was delighted to see the old man with the beard standing on the other side of the moat. The old man smiled when he could see recognition on the young elephant's face and he pulled the familiar white bag from his overcoat pocket. Siam flapped his ears at the visitor, noticing that he looked very tired, his eyes red and lined but looked otherwise healthy. No doubt, thought Siam, the winter had been difficult for the old man, too. But, with spring in the air and fairly recent news from Munich, his heart was happy. To the delight of his returning visitor, Siam raised a leg and trumpeted loudly, eliciting an equally contented reply from the nearby hippos. Soon, the whole zoo followed suit and the air was filled with the sounds of the animals welcoming the return of spring.

As spring progressed, Carl remained as disagreeable as ever, obviously valuing his dominant role over friendship. Siam, while angry at what he viewed as a betrayal, silently accepted things as they were and contented himself with the company of the females. Mary and Toni the Third, in turn, accepted the young bull, sensing his feelings of alienation from Carl. Neither of the females had ever understood the warring instincts of males, all surely the sons of Phi-ra. Nevertheless, Siam seemed different and, as a member of their rag-tag herd, the females felt it was their duty to include him in everything that they did. Perhaps, Mary secretly confided to Toni the Third, Siam was different from other males. In this one regard she was willing to discard the teachings of Ha. Surely, under such circumstances, the goddess would understand. Mary knew that, when musth, the time of male adulthood, arrived for Siam she might have to exert her dominance as matriarch. Until then she was content to wait.

She looked across the yard of the elephant house at her herd. As usual, Carl stood beside the old tree holding court. She smiled at the bull. No, as a female she could never understand the ways of males but, as an elephant, she knew that his behavior was to be expected. Siam and Kalifa played nearby, kicking a red rubber ball. Being considerably smaller than Siam, Kalifa the Second darted agilely around the bull, easily stealing the ball numerous times. Despite his age and size, Siam showed incredible patience with the baby and seemed to truly enjoy their little game. Toni the Third stood to one side, obviously amused by their antics, and she swayed from side to side expectantly, almost as if she wished to join in.

Smiling, Mary turned at the sound of a commotion behind her and inside of the elephant house. She raised her trunk and spied the metal door that separated the isolation room from their quarters open. Curious, she walked into the elephant house and approached the door, which was raised almost to the high ceiling by unseen pulleys. The spring air had made her forget herself and she felt like a young calf again, almost playful.

Mary could hear the voices of humans inside the chamber and gingerly approached the opening. Inside the chamber she could see humans in gray coveralls scrubbing the walls with brooms. Although she knew that she shouldn't have, Mary stuck her head through the opening, her curiosity propelling her forward. Although she felt her shoulder brush something hard she didn't hear the swift descent of the metal door. Only a sharp pain on the top of her head and the quick, frenzied expressions on the faces of the humans told her that something was terribly wrong. As rivulets of blood clouded her vision, she stumbled backwards into the stables and collapsed thunderously onto the concrete floor.

Carl, who had been watching from a distance, rushed to her side and shouted to Toni the Third to keep Kalifa the Second in the yard. He looked from Mary to the large metal door, which had somehow become detached and had landed squarely on Mary's head. Shouts on the other side of the metal door announced the arrival of the humans and Carl backed away warily as the man with the metal hook appeared once the door was reopened.

Siam stood in the doorway of the stables, unwilling to enter. Behind him, Kalifa the Second fought with Toni the Third, screaming for Mary. The sparrows, who had landed atop the metal bars of the open gate, cried out.

"Mary! Mary! Mary!"

In response, Mary groaned softly and could feel life slipping quickly from her. Through her shallow breaths, she instructed each of the elephants one last time.

Be fair.

Grow and be strong.

Remember that you're all a herd.

Take care of my baby.

And then, as had been and as still is, she whispered the

name that she had first whispered at birth and was gone.

Chapter Six

1935

The sudden death of Mary had a profound impact not only on the herd but on the entire zoo. Gorillas, hippos and chimpanzees offered condolences, and the birds stopped singing for an entire day. Even the sparrows seemed content to sit in their nests, high in the rafters, rather than scavenge for food. Toni the Third, suddenly thrust into the role of matriarch, seemed lost without Mary and did her best to watch over the orphaned Kalifa the Second. The baby, traumatized by Mary's death and the removal of her lifeless body, grew silent and no longer seemed interested in play. Only through the vigorous efforts of the older elephants was she persuaded to eat. Siam, for his part, had withdrawn even further. As far as he was concerned Mary was the third time that he had lost a mother, preceded by Su-ha and then Cora. It was only because of his concern for Kalifa the Second that he continued at all. Likewise, Carl was so moved by the loss of the matriarch that the role of dominant male seemed to have lost all importance. For him, with the loss of Carl, Mampe and Mary in such a short amount of time, it seemed as if it was the lot of captive elephants to constantly mourn. This realization filled him with a new-found generosity and he quickly reconciled with Siam, promising to never again take their friendship for granted.

Typical of the ever efficient humans, a new elephant was sent to the zoo a few months after the death of Mary. Whether or not she was meant as a replacement, a concept alien to elephant thinking, the others did their best to make the new arrival feel welcome. They knew, of course, that she was not there of her own free will and so was not responsible for any slight toward the memory of their fallen matriarch.

The new elephant, a four year old Asian female named Taku, was friendly and brought news from the Munich zoo where she had been taken after her capture in the wild. All of the elephants there, she had explained, were well, although the young bull, Wastl, was beginning to show the first signs of rebellion. This news cheered Siam, who was happy to hear that his old friend was showing signs of independence. The elephant Cora, she continued, had given birth to a baby boy named Seppl. The father, Boy, was as aggressive as ever and had, earlier in the year, attacked not only the elephant keeper there but also zoo director Heck. Otherwise, all was well.

***

Toni the Third gradually accepted her role as matriarch, and watched over Kalifa the Second as if she was her own. Kalifa the Second, too, finally seemed to accept her mother's death and had slowly emerged from her depression, encouraged by the help of the older elephants. Playing again in the courtyard with Siam seemed to have had a cathartic effect on the young cow. By the time spring once more came around, Mary had become nothing more than a revered memory, a precious object to guard and only bring out on special anniversaries. Taku had quickly fit in with the herd and, having been made privy to the situation of Mary's death, eagerly assisted Toni the Third in caring for Kalifa the Second.

Carl and Siam, their friendship rekindled, spent hours together each day beneath the old tree, just enjoying being males. Standing watch over the herd, they leaned on one another for both warmth and support and made a vow to be more vigilant against future threats to the herd. Never again, they agreed, could they allow another accident like the one that had befallen Mary or a depression to strike like the one that had destroyed Mampe. It was through this new-found alliance that the two bulls had arrived at a silent agreement that they would share the role of dominant male. The station was simply too much for one bull to manage. Similarly, Toni the Third and Taku seemed happy to share the responsibilities of matriarch and, for a year, all was peaceful in the elephant house.

***

Spring turned to summer and summer to fall and, as was inevitable, another winter came to the zoo. As in the wild, spring followed winter and the inhabitants of the zoo welcomed the return of warmth and longer days. Although none of the elephants could have known what was in store, the New Year brought many unexpected changes to the zoo. First, an odd thing was happening among the humans: all over the zoo, the words *"Nur fur Arier"* were being painted on every possible park bench in sight and the same words were painted on signs and affixed to posts. Although none of the elephants knew what the words meant, there was the general consensus that this new development was somehow bad. Siam observed the humans, who approached the benches with the cryptic messages and, based on his observations, guessed that some humans were allowed to sit on them, while others were inexplicably not. Again, he could detect no difference between the sitters and non-sitters, adding to his confusion surrounding the message on the benches.

Nevertheless, life at the zoo went on as normal. Then, in the fourth month, Aida, an Asian elephant arrived in Berlin from the zoo in Hannover. Aida, like Siam, had been born in the wild but refused to talk about her time before the humans had taken her or where she came from. Siam assumed, again, that the memories were perhaps too painful for her to recall so he forgave what might have been considered rudeness on the part of the newly arrived cow. But Aida was far from rude. In fact, she was very talkative and spoke for hours about her mate, Omar, who she had been forced to leave behind at the Hannover zoo. And, although she spoke fondly of Omar and even alluded to the day she would see him again, sadness in her eyes hinted that she knew that this would never be. Her one consolation, aside from being in the company of more elephants, was the fact that she was pregnant with Omar's unborn baby. The baby, who Aida hoped would be a male like its father, was not due for another twelve months. For the time being, she was relieved that the baby had survived the long journey to their new home and Toni the Third and Taku fretted over the new arrival as if she was royalty. Kalifa the Second, however, didn't seem overly impressed by the pregnant cow and maintained a silent distance. Whether or not she was less than thrilled at the prospect of the impending arrival of a new calf, a possibility that was highly unlikely, given the elephant's loyalty to the herd, or whether she was merely jealous of the attention Siam paid to the new arrival, Siam couldn't tell. Whatever the case Kalifa the Second was still mourning the death of her mother, Mary, and refused to discuss the matter whatsoever. One thing was certain, and the entire herd was in agreement: Aida talked far too much about her mate, Omar. While they all tried their best to include the new arrival in the herd and to treat her with kindness, they had each quickly learned to avoid being cornered by her. To do otherwise meant being forced to listen to endless stories about her paramour, by Aida's description the greatest elephant the world had ever seen, and risk the indignity of nodding off while she spoke. Both Taku and Toni the Third could easily excuse themselves from such conversations with the excuse of checking on the younger Kalifa the Second, and would carry their ruse to great lengths, checking every inch of the young female despite the fact that she had not been in distress in the first place. For Carl and Siam, however, there was no such excuse for escape and the two bulls took turns humoring the pregnant female. To make matters worse, Aida's stories of the great Omar made the two bulls feel horribly inadequate as males, not because of any criticisms but because Aida was clearly disinterested in either of them. Trying to mend his bruised ego, Carl assured Siam that Aida's lack of interest most likely stemmed from her pregnancy. It was a lie that Siam was all too happy to accept, although there was another matter had been keeping him preoccupied: his elderly human visitor had not appeared at the elephant pavilion for months, and Siam was worried that he might possibly have died. Or, worse, Siam imagined that the other humans had hurt him. Each night, as he drifted to sleep, Siam asked the goddess to protect the kind human.

***

The summer brought to the new arrivals to the elephant house, first Rani, a female Asian elephant who had been recently captured in the wild. Rani was only three years old, the same age as Siam had been when he was captured. These similarities endeared the young female to the older bull, and he kindly welcomed her into the herd although his attentions did not go unnoticed by Kalifa the Second. Her jealousy over Siam's interest in the new cow was compounded with the arrival of two new cows a month later. Korat, another Asian female arrived one afternoon along with Lindi, an African elephant who spoke proudly of her lost herd in Tanzania. Siam joked to Carl that, as the only two males at the elephant house, they were very fortunate to be surrounded by six females. Carl, however, didn't seem to find the humor in his friend's observations. For a week he had been complaining of stomach cramps and the humans in the white coats had visited the elephant house sometimes twice a day to visit him. Obviously ill, Carl had laughed off Siam's concern as unnecessary and assured his friend that he was merely feeling a bit under the weather as a result of the excitement caused by all of the new arrivals. But, when the humans, obviously unable to determine the cause of Carl's affliction, decided to quarantine him, Kalifa the Second became hysterical. To see Carl being led into the chamber where her father, Harry, had died and where her mother was accidentally killed was simply too much for her to bear. Taku and Toni the Third did their best to comfort Kalifa the Second and the newly arrived females, unaware of the history of the isolation chamber, stood aside and watched sadly as the young elephant wailed.

Siam knew that he would never see Carl again, as elephants can sense these sorts of things but, mostly for the benefit of Kalifa the Second, he wished Carl a speedy recovery. In reply, Carl joked with Siam, admonishing him to keep "their harem" safe until his return. Siam, whose face was suddenly wet, turned away as the door closed shut.

Carl, only fourteen seasons old, died that night. Upon learning this news, the elephants went about their traditional mourning period and even the new arrivals maintained a respectable silence in memory of the fallen African elephant. Nobody in the herd was as saddened, however, as Siam, who felt that he had lost his friend so soon after they had made peace with one another.

Incredibly, only a week after the death of Carl, news came

to the elephant house courtesy of the zoo grapevine: Bobby the gorilla, too, had died. Siam recalled Mampe's feigned dislike for the ape and chuckled despite the sadness he felt. As he stood at the edge of the elephant enclosure, Siam could hear the sounds of the other apes wailing from their enclosure. Strange, he thought, how different the customs of elephant and ape. Still, apes had been created by Ha just as the elephants had been, so there couldn't have been too much difference between them regarding the meaning of death. And, just like Carl, Bobby had died in captivity and far from his native home. If only for that reason, Siam decided, the old ape deserved to be mourned.

In reply to the cries of the apes, Siam trumpeted loudly, the sound carrying far over the grounds of the zoo.

Chapter Seven

1936

The following spring, during the fourth month, Aida gave birth to a baby boy who the zookeepers named Orje. The baby looked funny to Siam, covered in thick, fuzzy red hair but the females gathered around the infant and helped him to his feet, aiding him in his first meal outside of his mother's womb. As could have been predicted, they lavished all of their attention onto the new arrival, praising his size and beauty and, though it could hardly have been apparent at birth, his intelligence. Kalifa the Second, instead of being jealous as Siam had feared, seemed to take the new arrival in stride, warmed by the small creature's innocence and playful attitude. For Siam, who was still trying to get used to being the only male among the elephants, this was a welcome relief. And, with the birth of Orje came a frenzied burst of activity among the humans. Aida had at first mistaken the colorful banners and new construction outside the elephant enclosure as having been done in honor of her baby's safe birth. The other elephants, while amused by Aida's naïve assumption, were happy to allow her this one fantasy, nevertheless. In truth, none of them knew what all of the activity was about, and the colorful banner that hung between two poles nearby offered no clues. Just above five linked circles of blue, yellow, black green and red were painted the words "*Wilkommen Olympische Spiel*." And, creating even more confusion for the elephants, the cryptic message that had been painted on the park benches and signs was suddenly painted over, the message magically eradicated with a few strokes of a paint brush. Adding to the odd atmosphere, more colorful uniforms appeared at the zoo. These men wore light brown breeches and tunics with shiny, brown boots. On their sleeves were tiny versions of the banners and the tunics were adorned with all manner of silver and gold. Siam thought that they must be royalty but Toni the Third, who disliked the haughty air of these men, joked that they looked like peacocks strutting around. The best thing about this activity was that the humans in the brown uniforms stopped harassing other humans, as if suddenly on their best behavior. None of the elephants could explain this sudden behavioral change but hoped that it would last.

Siam and the other elephants watched as workers scurried here and there, attaching more of the red, white and black banners to every pole imaginable, all under the watchful eye of the zoo director. The word circulating around the zoo, and which eventually found its way to the elephant house, was that the zoo director was building a new exhibit on the zoo grounds, this one dedicated solely to animals native to the region. Bears, lynxes and otters were to be the stars of the exhibit although none of the elephants could understand why this was such an honor, considering that even the native animals were still behind bars. Siam decided to leave such speculation to the females of the herd, however. But the activity brought many new visitors to the zoo, humans who looked different than the pale-skinned, straw haired captors. By the summer, the zoo was filled with dark-skinned visitors and humans that reminded Siam of his homeland. Many different languages could be heard among the humans and the sparrows repeated the names of places like Bolivia, Chile and India.

Whatever the cause for the activity, Siam was simply disinterested. Already in his fifteenth season, Siam had more personal concerns to attend to, namely that his body was transforming into that of a fully grown male. Musth was upon him and his sexual urges were almost too much to bear. The fact that none of the females seemed interested in mating only made matters worse and Siam seemed to be constantly sporting an erection. Kalifa the Second, only eight years old, was horribly confused by the changes in Siam and giggled constantly at Siam's embarrassing physical condition. Humiliated, Siam often took refuge in the solitude of the stables, far away from prying eyes. It was one afternoon, while hiding in the stables, that he received good news from Toni the Third, who called to him excitedly. Siam walked warily to the door and looked at the cow who was smiling at him broadly. He was about to turn and walk back into the shelter of the stables, certain that Toni the Third was only trying to coax him outside out of pity. But, with a sway of her trunk, she pointed outside the enclosure. Siam gazed just past her and saw that a lone human stood on the walk, an expectant look on his face. Filled with curiosity, Siam stepped out into the sunlight and walked to the edge of the moat. Although the old man was now shorn of his white beard and his skin was an almost translucent white, there was no mistaking his old friend. As if no time had passed, the old human pulled a familiar paper bag from his coat and, glancing from side to side, cautiously tossed a handful of peanuts to Siam. Siam, so excited to see his old friend, ignored the offering and trumpeted loudly and raised one foot off of the ground. Kalifa the Second joined Siam at the edge of the moat and snatched up a trunk full of peanuts, to the delight of the old man, who clapped his hands and smiled gleefully. He stood watching the elephants until, to Siam's dismay, two men in the brown uniforms approached and he quickly scurried away, despite the fact that they seemed disinterested in him. Siam trumpeted a goodbye and glared at the uniformed men, who stood before the elephant enclosure for a moment before continuing on. Despite his anger at the uniformed men, Siam was amazed at the sudden reappearance of the old man. Had the goddess, Ha, resurrected him from the dead? Was this even possible? Siam wasn't sure, but kept his thoughts to himself. Perhaps, if the goddess had resurrected the old man, she could also bring back Carl or even his mother. He closed his eyes, the sun on his face, and made his secret request.

Then, as if by unseen magic, the marching bands, the foreign visitors and the banners with the colorful circles disappeared before the end of the month. Within days all of these things were replaced with the cryptic message, which reappeared on the zoo's benches.

***

The following April brought more new arrivals to the elephant house. First, a seven year old wild born, Asian elephant named Birma, had been sent to Berlin from the Hamburg zoo. Siam was instantly smitten with the vivacious Birma and flirted with her shamelessly, offering her bits of melon and extra hay. Though she seemed oblivious to the male's advances, Kalifa the Second took special notice, and became testy whenever Birma came near. Toni the Third, acting the role of matriarch, scolded Kalifa the Second and offered apologies to Birma. As a result, Kalifa the Second began to ignore Siam instead, retreating to the safety of the other females any time he came near her. For a while, the older bull mistook Kalifa the Second's attitude as a simple matter of misunderstood youth but, when Kalifa the Second continued to ignore him he turned to Toni the Third for clues. When she laughed at the bull's naïveté and explained the reason behind the youngster's actions, Siam wrinkled his brow in confusion.

"How," he asked, "can Kalifa the Second be jealous when she has no interest in mating? Besides," he grumbled, "there is nothing between me and Birma; therefore Kalifa the Second's jealousy is doubly ridiculous."

Toni the Third could only smile knowingly as Siam lumbered slowly across the courtyard mumbling to himself.

***

A month later, the Asian female, Rani, was suddenly prodded into the isolation room by the man with the iron hook. The rest of the elephants were horribly confused by this sudden intrusion into their routine. For one thing, Rani was not sick and so there was no reason to isolate her.

Secondly, she got along well with the other elephants, always kept to herself and had never been aggressive to their human handlers, so her sudden isolation made no sense, whatsoever. When a lorry suddenly appeared outside the elephant house with the words "*Zoo Hamburg*" chalked on its side, however, it suddenly became clear to the others what was happening to Rani.

Kalifa the Second commented that the humans were awful for taking elephants whenever they felt like doing so.

> "None of us should be here in the first place," commented Siam, though he quickly let the matter drop. What could Kalifa, an elephant born in a zoo, understand about true freedom?

Kalifa ignored Siam's strange comment. What did he mean "none of us should be here?" Where else would they be so well-taken care of? Still, she couldn't comprehend how their captors could move them from place to place, with no respect for elephant customs. In her anger toward the humans she forgot her jealousy and pressed her body against Siam. Heartened by this, Siam trumpeted a loud goodbye to Rani. Toni the Third wished her well and thanked her for her friendship. The sentiment was echoed by Lindi, Korat, Birma, Taku and Aida. The group stood crowded in the far corner of the enclosure and watched as Rani was prodded onto the back of the lorry. As soon as the gate on the back slammed shut with a loud clang and a metal latch was firmly in place, they all turned, one by one, and returned to the courtyard.

That November, on their noisy migration north, the crows arrived, bearing news. Two crows, which arrived just after feeding time, landed to pick up scattered bits of food from the concrete, once again displacing the sparrows, which took flight and resettled atop Siam's back. Siam recognized one as Yach, whom he had met the previous spring and he inquired as to the whereabouts of his friend, Blach. Yach shook his head sadly, and explained that Blach had gone to eternal sleep in a field in the south. His new companion, a crow named Skeech, bowed his head reverently. Siam apologized and offered his condolences to the noisy birds. He conveyed to them the news of the deaths of Carl and Mary, news that he knew they would carry to other zoos. Yach flew up and landed on Siam's back, followed by Skeech. The sparrows, incensed by this second breach of protocol, took to the bare tree. Yach ignored them and cheerfully announced that not all was bad news: at the Munich zoo, he explained, the elephant Mini had given birth to a girl named Stasi. The proud Boy, he said, was the father. Toni the Third, who was standing nearby, overheard the news and trumpeted loudly, happy that another elephant baby, like Kalifa the Second, had been born in the safety of a zoo. As Yach and Skeech thanked the elephants for the food and made their noisy departure, headed for the nearby park, Siam thanked them for the good news.

Chapter Eight

1938

The camaraderie that was rekindled between Kalifa the Second and Siam on the occasion of Rani's **sudden** departure lasted just over a year. Through the spring, the summer and into the fall the young female became more and more withdrawn, choosing instead the company of the other females over the company of her former friend, Siam. Siam, in turn, had been forced to gradually accept this turn of events and soon forgot all about Kalifa the **Second**'s fickle nature.

As with every fall since Siam's arrival, the crows arrived at the zoo. Although he recognized his old friend, Yach, and Yach's new companion, Skeech, they bore little news of the outside world. The only interesting tidbit they brought was that Boy, still at the Munich zoo, was as aggressive as ever and had been placed in isolation. Otherwise, little else had changed; the baby, Stasi, was healthy and growing and Wastl was becoming an adult. Siam thanked the crows for their news and once again bade them farewell.

By early winter musth was finally upon Siam. His head ached as the hormones inside his body wrought havoc on him and a thick, potent secretion stained his checks and ran into his mouth, creating what felt like the worst toothache in the world. He ground his tusks into the earth in an unsuccessful attempt to alleviate his discomfort. To make matters worse, a steady stream of urine trickled down his hind quarters, causing the skin to become irritated and sore. The zookeepers, suddenly wary of the aggressive young bull, decided it best to separate him from the rest of the herd and placed him in a neighboring pen, closed off from the females. It wasn't as if the humans would not have welcomed another baby elephant but bulls, especially at musth, were known to kill, and the last thing that the zoo director wanted was to have one of his prized females injured or killed. It was decided, therefore, to isolate Siam and until one of the females was ready to mate. Fortunately, the isolation pen was not the same chamber he had been placed in upon his arrival at the zoo. This pen, used exclusively for such reasons, was much bigger than the original isolation chamber, had its own small yard and separated Siam from the females with only a barred gate. It was through this gate that the human handlers cautiously fed and watered the young bull.

But, being the only male and separated from the herd, Siam grew sullen, tipping over water brought for him, ignoring the food placed in front of him and, once, swinging his massive trunk at the man with the iron rod.

The handler, of course, brought the *ankus* smashing down onto Siam's trunk as punishment but Siam refused to show remorse. Why, he wondered, his mind racing, should he care to live or die when he had been moved from the herd? This was his punishment, simply because his body was playing a cruel joke on him. As soon as the man with the iron rod had gone Siam picked up a melon and tossed it toward the rafters with great force. It shattered, narrowly missing one of the sparrow's nests, and the birds squawked their disapproval at the humiliated bull. There he remained, alone and cold, throughout the long and bitter winter.

***

By the time the first leaves began to appear on the trees the following year, the effects of musth subsided, Siam was once again allowed back into the courtyard with the females. As he emerged, hungry for the warmth of the early spring sunlight, he felt humiliated as he passed the silent females. He stopped beside the tree and looked across the moat, out over the rest of the zoo. It was Toni the Third, the matriarch, who first approached him, though she did so cautiously. Her voice low so that the others couldn't hear, she asked if he was feeling better.

"Much," replied Siam, though he found that he couldn't meet the female's gaze. "What news of the zoo in my absence?"

Toni the Third smiled, amused by Siam's theatrics. Even though he had been shut away in a separate enclosure, he had still been on zoo grounds and could have easily learned of any news. Nevertheless, she knew that he had suffered and had truly missed him. She replied that there was no news to report and that the routine had been fairly boring in his absence. This kindness stirred the young bull's heart and he touched Toni the Third's trunk with his own.

"It wasn't your fault," she said, softly. "It is what all males are doomed to suffer."

Siam nodded, but his face remained solemn. For the first time since musth, he understood the goddess' commandment regarding the separation of males from females. At least here, he wryly noted, he had been allowed to return whereas, in the wild, he would only see his friends perhaps once or twice a year.

Toni the Third implored Siam to join the others but he declined, explaining that he was finally an adult and, as the dominant male, must begin to act as such. Toni the Third grudgingly agreed but reminded Siam of one important thing.

"We are a herd," she said. "And everyone within the herd remains loyal to the herd."

Siam assured Toni the Third of his loyalty but decided to remain beside his tree, nevertheless. As the matriarch ambled away to rejoin the other females, Siam looked out over the grounds of the zoo. He was the dominant male, the only male, and he was now an adult.

***

The following month, at the height of spring, another elephant arrived at the zoo. There was much discussion among the elephants regarding the new arrival, primarily regarding food shortages.

"We don't need another elephant," grumbled Korat. "How can the humans **manage to feed so many animals?**"

Aida agreed.

> "If there isn't enough food," she said, twining her trunk around Orje, "how am I supposed to feed my little one?"

There was the general murmur of agreement from the other females, but Toni the Third remained silent.

> "The new arrival is an elephant," she finally said, her voice soft, "and, as such, we must offer her our hospitality."

Aida looked embarrassed and it was Taku who spoke next.

> "You're right, of course. After all, I'm sure our new arrival doesn't want to be here any more than we do."

Again silence fell over the herd.

"Why do the humans move us from place to place?" asked Birma.

"For their own amusement," replied Siam, briefly glancing in their direction before resuming his watch over the zoo grounds.

The females turned, startled by Siam's sudden interjection into their conversation, but none of them dared to contradict the bull. How could they? They all knew that there was a grain of truth in what he said and had, in fact, suspected as much.

The new elephant was called Tembo by the humans, and was a female African elephant that had been shipped to Berlin from the zoo in Cologne. After the customary period of isolation the new female timidly emerged from her solitary chamber and into the sunlight. She looked warily around at her new surroundings and, following elephant custom she greeted Toni the Third, her head low and the tip of her trunk in the matriarch's mouth. Toni the Third introduced her to the others as they gathered around the new arrival. Even Kalifa the Second stopped playing with the baby, Orje, in order to get a look at the new female. Confused by his playmate's sudden disinterest, Orje joined his mother, Aida, who pulled the baby close. Toni the Third introduced Aida, Taku, Korat, Lindi and Birma, saving Kalifa the Second and Orje for last due to their age. As greetings were acknowledged and returned, Toni the Third turned to Siam, who had remained beside his tree.

"This is Siam," she said, addressing Tembo, "our male."

At these words Siam's ears perked up. Had he heard correctly? Had Toni the Third actually referred to him as "our male?" He felt his heart swell with pride. Despite the fact that he was well aware of his status within the herd, he had never heard the matriarch honor him in such a way. Suddenly, the silly humans watching him from outside the enclosure didn't seem to matter. Deeply moved, Siam approached the new female and nearly tripped in his haste, eliciting a giggle from Kalifa the Second. Toni the Third quickly silenced the youngster with a pointed look, although Siam didn't seem to have noticed.

Although she was much larger than Siam, Tembo greeted the male politely. Siam sputtered a shy welcome, ignoring the amused faces of the other females, and then returned to his tree.

As the females bombarded Tembo with questions regarding the world outside of the zoo, Siam let out a contented sigh. The last time he had been around so many females was in the wild, when he had been protected by his aunts, sisters and mother. Suddenly, Siam missed his old friend, Carl, who surely would have loved being surrounded by so many females. What had he called it, a harem? Siam smiled at the joke and leaned heavily against the tree, as if it was his old friend, Carl.

***

As is bound to happen, spring slowly faded from its pastel glory into the less subtle and warmer summer. The transition occurred so slowly, in fact, that Siam almost missed nature's little hints. But being locked up in an artificial place like a zoo, it was easy to lose touch with such things and the ragtag herd of elephants at the Berlin zoo was beginning to suffer from the tedium of captivity. For those born in the wild, which was all of the elephants except for Orje and Kalifa the Second, the youngest elephants, life behind bars was enough to extinguish the soul. Siam, in particular, was showing signs of strain despite the fact that he had been deprived of his freedom since childhood. Everyday, his routine was the same;

awaken from five hours of sleep, eat, pace the courtyard, nap, eat, pace the courtyard, stand beside the tree to amuse the humans, pace the courtyard, eat and then back to sleep. It wasn't as if he was deprived of life's petty amusements, the constant chatter of the females, passed news from other animals in the zoo and the play of the young Kalifa the Second and the baby Orje, but food and shelter only went so far in meeting the young bull's needs. Was it too much for him to want to walk farther than the zoo's walls allowed? Siam looked north, in the direction of the trees that comprised the nearby park, and longed to walk beneath their leafy canopies, if only for one afternoon. Knowing that this could never happen, Siam contented himself with another circuit around the courtyard.

***

It was during the eighth month, in the midst of a particularly humid summer that the baby, Orje, suddenly died. Although his mother, Aida, had noticed that his appetite had diminished she had attributed this to the sweltering heat. When the humans came to take the lifeless body away Aida fought them back with the ferocity of a lioness, even enduring the blows of the metal rod in her attempt to keep Orje with her. Moved and impressed by her bravery, the other females joined her and created an impenetrable wall that none of the human handlers dared approach. To the elephant's amazement, their act of resistance worked and the humans, visibly confounded, left the dead elephant alone. By the third day, however, concerned because Aida refused to leave her dead child even to eat, Toni the Third approached her.

"You must eat, Aida," she said, her voice soft.

"If I feed then the humans will take Orje from me," she replied, her eyes vacant.

"Orje is already gone," replied the matriarch. "Perhaps it is time for us to let him go."

Aida jerked her head, a crazed expression on her face, but Toni the Third silenced her with a gentle growl.

"He is with the goddess now," she said. "We must allow the humans to remove his remains."

"But where will they take him?" asked Aida, large tears running down her lined face. "How will I be able to honor him?"

Toni the Third didn't reply; this was the quandary of elephants in captivity, the inability to know where their loved ones were taken after death. Toni the Third looked at the fuzzy baby, covered with flies, and then back at his grieving mother.

"Come with me," she said.

Reluctantly, Aida followed her to the far end of the courtyard, leaving Orje alone. The first step was the most difficult, for she knew that she was letting Orje go. Nevertheless, she followed the matriarch and each step seemed to be easier than the first. The other females, in an attempt to offer support, followed. Siam, however, remained beside the tree and refused to look at the dead baby. When the humans appeared shortly thereafter, however, obviously tipped off to this new development, Siam trumpeted loudly. The humans paused, wary of the bull but, when it became obvious that he would remain beside the tree, the men hauled the carcass onto a wagon. The flies, which had begun making a home of the corpse, took flight in a great swarm and one of the men vomited.

One of his comrades laughed rudely but, he, too, maintained a look of utter disgust.

With great effort they pushed the cart into the elephant house and through the sliding door, forgetting to close the gate behind them. Siam hesitated for a moment but, when it became evident that the men had not noticed their blunder, Siam saw his opportunity. Quickly, he ran into the elephant house and peered through the opening and into the isolation chamber. Mindful of the accident that had felled Mary at the door, Siam peered cautiously through, careful not to get too close.

Outside the door of the chamber, in the sunlight, a lorry sat idling. The men were wrestling Orje's little body onto the back of the lorry when, suddenly, the human who had vomited, turned to see Siam standing in the door. His face turned white and he rushed to the door, which he slammed shut with a loud bang, but not before Siam had seen writing on the side of the lorry.

"Rudnitz."

What did it mean? Siam turned and walked back into the courtyard, where the females remained huddled at one end. Could Rudnitz be a place? And, if it was a place, was this where the humans took the elephant dead for burial? Siam growled, angrily. If only the crows were there. It was a question he would ask them on their next visit. He wrote the word in the dirt beneath his feet, using his trunk and Kalifa the Second joined him and looked inquisitively at his handiwork.

"What is that?" she asked.

Siam looked at the young female with sadness in his eyes.

"Tell Aida I have found Orje's resting place."

***

Sadly, the strange illness that killed the baby, Orje, also claimed the lives of Taku and Korat. Like Orje, the two females stopped eating and quickly succumbed to the strange malady. The humans moved the two sick cows into the isolation chamber, first Korat and then Taku. There they both died after three days in isolation. The remainder of the herd was filled with fear. What sort of sickness, they wondered amongst themselves, was killing them off?

Again, in both instances, Siam observed the lorry and its strange markings: *Rudnitz*.

As the lorry drove away, belching foul smelling fumes into the warm air, Siam turned to the females.

"At least we know where our friends are going," he said, tears staining his wrinkled cheeks.

"Rudnitz," sobbed Kalifa the Second.

"Rudnitz," whispered Toni the Third, her head bowed in reverence.

"Rudnitz! Rudnitz! Rudnitz!" echoed a trio of sparrows, who were perched in the nearby tree.

Siam approached the tree and looked at the sparrows.

"Do you know Rudnitz?" he asked.

Although quite talkative, Siam had learned that the sparrows could be quite unreliable for information. Unlike the crows, they tended to contradict one another, even on the smallest points.

"Dog food! Dog food! Dog food!" they chirped.

It took a moment for Siam to digest what the birds had said. He had, of course, seen the domesticated dogs of humans, lower creatures than even tigers, in Siam's opinion, because of their pathetic loyalty to their human masters. Once he had regained his composure, however, Siam pressed the tiny birds for more information.

"What do you mean?" he asked, his voice almost a whisper.

"Dog food!" they repeated.

Siam swung his trunk at the branch, causing the sparrows to scatter in the air. He had known better than to ask the sparrows for information; clearly they were playing a cruel trick on him. He would simply have to wait another month or so for the crows to return. Then he would get the information that he needed. Angry, he turned back to the gathered females.

"What was that all about?" asked **Toni the Third**.

"Nothing," lied Siam.

If the sparrows were right it would be the worst desecration imaginable for an elephant, and Siam refused to share this rumor with the mourning herd, particularly Aida, who had so recently lost her baby, Orje. The humans could be cruel, but surely not this cruel.

No, Siam thought, the sparrows were merely lying.

A day later, Aida was moved into the isolation chamber. Still deeply mourning the loss of Orje, she offered no resistance. The herd bade her farewell, certain they would never see her again. But they were all surprised when she emerged, seemingly well, two days later.

> "They did all kinds of tests," she explained, her spirits low. "I suppose they thought that I had the illness, too."

> "We're just glad that you're back," replied Toni the Third.

The herd gathered around Aida and touched her with their trunks, as if to verify that she had truly returned.

***

Shortly after the sudden deaths of Orje, Taku and Korat, two new elephants came to the zoo. Tembo, a wild born African elephant, arrived from the Cologne zoo followed by Taku the Second, a wild born Asian female, from the zoo in Warsaw. Although the herd was horribly offended by Taku the Second's name, a clear case of disrespect for the dead Taku on the part of the humans, Siam was instantly smitten by her. Finally, he thought, he might have found his mate. They were certainly compatible, both Asian elephants, both wild born and both around the same age. The rest of the herd, sensing Siam's interest, quickly forgave the new arrival for her name. Besides, they reasoned, the name had been given her by the humans. None of their names were their given, elephant names, so why should they blame Taku the Second for this callous joke?

To Siam's great surprise, Taku the Second seemed to share his interest and, although their courtship was a slow, winding dance, the new cow flirted with the bull in such an obvious way that there was no mistaking her intentions. All through the summer Taku the Second followed Siam around the enclosure like a school girl, casting furtive glances in his direction and giggling like a parrot when he returned her attention. The other females of the herd watched this unfolding with a mixture of amusement and relief, relief because it meant that Siam would leave them in peace once musth was upon him again and amusement because it was clear that the bull had never mated. Toni the Third quieted the other female's chatter, happy to see that Siam might have found his mate. Kalifa the Second, however, was obviously unhappy at this new development. Although she still had no interest in mating with the bull, she was made jealous by the sudden lack of attention paid her by Siam and retreated whenever Taku the Second appeared.

One afternoon, when the leaves on the trees had already begun to turn the color of the sun, Siam got his first clear invitation from Taku the Second. He was already suffering the early stages of musth and, irritated by the steady stream of urine, which trickled down his hind legs, had retreated to a far corner of the enclosure to be alone. As he stood there watching the antics of two butterflies, dancing and spiraling in the air before him, he heard the unmistakable sound of a female in estrus. He placed a foot squarely on the ground and raised his ears. This time the sound was louder and more pronounced. Excited, Siam rounded the elephant house and spied Taku the Second, separated from the other females, standing beside the tree. He approached cautiously and she smiled and touched the male with her trunk. Although Siam had never mated, his instincts told him what to do and he walked behind Taku the Second and touched her opening with his trunk. It was wet, a good sign, and he placed his trunk in his mouth. The taste confirmed that she was, indeed, in estrus. Siam's heart was racing and he ambled back to the semi-privacy of the far side of the elephant house. Taku the Second followed. With a reassuring rumble, Siam mounted the cow from behind. She opened up for him willingly and Siam marveled at the sensation of the female's warmth. The butterflies continued their spiral dance, although Siam had ceased to pay them any attention. When the brief session was over, the two elephants stood with their trunks intertwined for a very long time, touching and caressing one another, as the sunlight through the tree leaves dappled their skin and warmed them.

This is freedom, Siam thought, even if I am in a zoo.

* * *

One night, early in the eleventh month, with Taku the Second sleeping beside him, Siam was awakened from his light sleep by the sound of movement. In the semi-darkness of the elephant house, he spied Kalifa the Second, standing alone and peering out into the courtyard. Careful not to awaken the other elephants, Siam joined her at the barred gate.

"What's the matter?" he whispered. "Can't you sleep?"

Kalifa the Second didn't look at Siam.

"What do you care?" she asked, staring into the darkness.

Siam was taken aback by this sudden burst of anger.

"Have I done something wrong?"

Kalifa jerked her head in Siam's direction, her eyes flashing, and then looked back toward the zoo grounds.

"Is this about Taku the Second?" he asked, his voice low.

"Does everything have to be about her?" snapped Kalifa the Second.

Although she hadn't directly answered his question, Siam felt as if he had received one.

"She's really nice," he said. "You should give her a chance."

"You don't get it, do you?" said Kalifa the Second.

Before Siam could reply, the sounds of breaking glass and humans shouting filled the air. The noise wasn't coming from inside the zoo but outside, on the streets. The two elephants raised their ears in an attempt to better hear. The one word that Siam kept hearing repeated was one that he didn't understand.

Jude.

When the noise had quieted, obviously moving farther away, he turned to Kalifa the Second but she had returned to her corner and was feigning sleep. Frustrated by their brief exchange and confused by the commotion on the street, Siam returned to Taku the Second's side and drifted into a fitful sleep.

The next morning the smell of smoke filled the chilly air and, although there was general agreement among the zoo's animals that something had happened the night before, nobody seemed to know exactly what had happened. Only the sparrows seemed to offer any additional clues, squawking in unison.

"Kristallnacht! Kristallnacht! Kristallnacht!"

Already angry at them over the Rudnitz remark, Siam ignored them and didn't pursue the matter.

Later that month saw the arrival of the migrating crows. Although he was afraid of what he might learn, he was determined to learn what he could of the place called Rudnitz. He was happy to see his friend Yach and his partner, Skeech, picking at scraps on the ground and approached them with a loud trumpet.

Yach looked momentarily annoyed but, when he recognized Siam, squawked a reply and hopped on the elephant's back. As was customary, Siam passed on the news of their recent deaths and new arrivals to the zoo, news that the crows would pass along to other zoos on their migration. Yach, in turn, passed on what he had heard on the outside, although the bulk of his information came from the zoo in Munich. After a brief moment of silence, Siam mustered the courage to ask the question he had been waiting to ask.

"Yach," he asked hesitantly, "have you ever heard of a place called Rudnitz?"

Yach squawked loudly and flew down to the ground.

"No," he lied, busying himself with bits of grain on the ground, "never."

"Good eats," said Skeech, unaware of his mistake.

Yach squawked loudly at Skeech and flew at him, causing Skeech to retreat to the roof of the elephant house. He turned back to Siam and apologized for his companion's insensitivity.

"Why do you ask of this place?" he asked.

"Do they take elephants there after they die?" asked Siam.

Yach sighed, defeated.

"All animals," he said, his head bowed. "Once they have died, all animals from the zoo go to this place."

Siam quickly explained what the sparrows had said.

Yach clucked his tongue and shook his head.

"You mustn't listen to sparrows," he said. "They talk too much."

"But, is it true?" asked Siam. "Do they make us into dog food?"

Realizing that his friend already knew the truth, Yach merely nodded. Siam stared at the crow, dumbfounded.

"Take care, my friend," said Yach. He was clearly saddened by the conversation and suddenly took flight, rejoining Skeech in a noisy reunion on the roof of the elephant house.

"What was that all about?"

Siam turned to see Aida, standing behind him, her expression somewhere between inquisitive and amused.

"Nothing," he lied. He quickly turned to go and find Taku the Second.

***

The next month a new arrival came to the elephant house, only this time it was a familiar face. Jenny the Second arrived from the Hannover zoo with her baby,

Indra, born only a month before. Jenny the Second had been friends with Aida when she was there and the two females greeted each other warmly. Jenny the Second explained that Indra had been sired by Omar, Aida's former paramour in Hannover and Aida sadly explained that her baby, Orje, also sired by Omar, had died a few months earlier. Jenny the Second was obviously embarrassed by her gaffe and offered her sincere condolences.

"You can help me raise Indra," she offered. "That is what we elephants do, after all."

Tears quickly stained Aida's cheeks and she looked at the fuzzy baby, so like her little Orje.

"I promise," she said. "I won't let anything happen to your little one."

Siam watched all of this from a distance. Although winter was coming, he felt warm inside. He was the only bull among all of the females, they were well taken care of and he finally had a mate of his own. And, he noted with pride, it was only a matter of time, perhaps, before he and Taku the Second had a baby, too.

Chapter Nine

1939

Although the winter passed not unlike the previous winters of his stay at the Berlin zoo, it seemed far more pleasant than any Siam could recall. And, since he was blessed, like all elephants, with an excellent memory, he was certain of it. The new cows, Taku the Second, Tembo, Jenny the Second and her baby, Indra, were quickly accepted into the herd by the other females. Even Aida, busy in the task of assisting with Indra, seemed to have forgotten the loss of her own baby, Orje. Only Kalifa the Second seemed to resist accepting the new arrivals, particularly Taku the Second. Siam, on more than one occasion, tried to speak with the young cow in an effort to understand her rude behavior, but she rebuffed him each time he approached her. One afternoon, when there was still snow on the ground, Siam attempted to speak with her after witnessing a heated exchange between the two cows. As usual, Kalifa retreated to the other end of the courtyard and refused to speak with the bull. He started after her but was stayed by Toni the Second.

"Leave her alone," she said.

"But I don't understand her behavior," Siam protested. "Why does she not accept you?"

Toni the Second smiled.

"You truly are a male," she said, not unkindly. "Don't you know that she loves you?"

Siam laughed, certain that this was a joke, but Toni the Third, who was standing nearby, spoke.

"It's true, Siam," she said. "She has loved you for a very long time. Didn't you know?"

The other females concurred and Siam suddenly felt very foolish.

"But Kalifa the Second has always been like a sister to me," he said.

"Nevertheless," replied Toni the Third, "you must give her time to accept Taku the Second. There is no way to rush the mending of a broken heart."

Siam looked across the courtyard and saw Kalifa the Second, standing alone near the fence.

"What should I do?" he asked, his heart heavy.

"Just give her time," replied Toni the Third. "She will eventually get over this."

Siam looked back at the forlorn cow and slowly nodded his consent. What could he do? Certainly the females of the herd knew better than he the working of the female heart.

***

As the weather slowly warmed more and more humans returned to the zoo. Siam observed the visitors from his spot beside the tree and noticed that new uniforms were beginning to appear. While he was used to seeing the gaudy uniforms of the men in brown, adorned with all manner of shiny and colorful decorations, the striking black uniforms of the men who sported lightning bolts on their collars and even the human young, dressed in all manner of miniature replicas of their adult counterparts, late winter brought new, austere versions. These new uniforms, while still covered with ribbons and decorations, were simpler than the ones usually seen. Shades of dark green, dark blue and light blue began to appear and Siam couldn't help but wonder what the human fascination with clothing could mean. And, although he searched the crowds for any sign of his elderly friend, he had begun to fear the worst, namely that the humans had killed him or that he had simply vanished.

One afternoon, as Siam looked for his friend among a crowd of people just outside the elephant enclosure, Taku the Second joined him and asked him what he was doing. Siam quickly explained to his mate this situation with the elderly human; his kindness, the peanuts and the humans who clearly disliked him for no apparent reason. Touched by Siam's concern, Taku the Second twined her trunk in his.

"You're sweet," she said and pressed her body close to his.

Siam, surprised by this reaction to his story, forgot about the old human and reciprocated. As the two elephants swayed affectionately together beneath the tree Kalifa the Second approached the moat that separated the elephants from the humans. The humans smiled at the young female, attention which emboldened the young cow. In an attempt to take Siam's attention away from Taku the Second, Kalifa the Second climbed onto the lip of the moat and gingerly executed a tight rope walk along the edge. The humans, amused by this spontaneous bit of entertainment, applauded, snapping Siam from his amorous thoughts.

"Kalifa," he bellowed, "get down from there...the wall is slippery from the ice!"

Kalifa the Second giggled. For once she was in the spotlight and it was exhilarating.

"Kalifa!" snarled Siam. "Get down from there, you stupid little girl!"

Startled by Siam's sudden gruffness, Kalifa the Second looked at him in shock before tumbling into the deep moat. The humans looked shocked and two of their females screamed. The rest of the herd rushed to the edge of the moat and peered down into it, where Kalifa the Second stood, dazed. Her bloody footprints led back to the spot where she had landed, atop the metal spikes placed in the bottom of the moat to discourage escape attempts. Otherwise, Kalifa the Second appeared unharmed and cried up to the other elephants for assistance.

"Get me out of here," she wailed.

Siam leaned over the edge and offered his trunk to the wounded female.

"Grab hold," he said, trying his best to remain calm. Siam and the other elephants knew that an elephant with a wounded foot was in grave danger of infection, but the important thing was to remain calm. Kalifa the Second reached for Siam's trunk with her own but missed. She slipped back into the moat and onto the spikes. Copious amounts of blood were beginning to pool in the moat at her feet and Siam was attempting to reach back in when he heard a commotion behind him. He turned and saw that the man with the iron rod had entered the courtyard, his face ashen. He was followed by four men with ropes and wooden planks. Hastily, the man with the iron rod began herding the other elephants into the elephant house. Siam hesitated when approached but reasoned that the humans could probably rescue Kalifa the Second far more easily than he. He quickly joined the others and watched as the humans, using their ropes and planks of wood, finally managed to haul the elephant back to the courtyard. Again the humans on the other side of the moat cheered and Siam was inclined to agree. But, as the wounded Kalifa limped past, leaving bloody footprints in her wake, Siam prayed to the goddess to spare his young friend.

Sensing Siam's fears, Taku the Second pressed against him.

"She will be fine," she whispered. "The humans take very good care of us here."

"Then why do they place those spikes at the bottom of the moat?" snapped Siam. "If it wasn't for those she wouldn't be hurt as badly...only a couple of bruises!"

Hurt by his sudden outburst, Taku the Second recoiled.

"I'm sorry," she said, tears forming in her eyes. "I know that she is your friend."

Siam quickly apologized to his mate and rushed to the door of the isolation chamber, where the humans had taken the injured cow.

"Kalifa," Siam shouted through the metal door. He had surprised himself by shortening her name, an act of familiarity. "Are you alright?"

"No," came the muffled reply. "I hurt."

"Kalifa," Siam continued, "let the humans help you…they will make you better."

"I will," Kalifa the Second replied. Then, after a brief pause, "Siam, I'm sorry for the way I've been acting."

Siam silenced her with a low rumble.

"Just get better," he said.

He turned and rejoined the other elephants, which were silently milling about the courtyard, their faces serious. Toni the Third was sniffing at the blood on the ground, while the baby, Indra, played as if nothing had happened.

Siam looked back across the moat and saw that the humans had dispersed, obviously having gotten enough entertainment for the day. He stood beside Taku the Second and pressed his body against hers as an apology.

***

Kalifa the Second remained in the isolation chamber for a week and, although the herd was unable to see her, they spoke to her through the vast expanse of the metal door and offered words of encouragement. Siam, in particular, felt responsible for the accident. If he hadn't barked at her, would Kalifa the Second fallen into the moat? He visited her daily, speaking through the door. Her voice was weak but her spirits were good, and Siam was confident that this meant that she would be returning to the herd soon.

***

A week after the accident, as the herd stood sleeping, Siam had a dream. In it, he was back in his native land walking in the jungle; his mother was there as were his sisters and aunts. As they walked through the brush the herd stopped. A few feet in front of them stood a little girl, a human. Her skin was olive colored and her dark hair was twisted into a bun atop her head. She wore a traditional sari and held in her hands a bright pink lotus blossom. She approached Siam and held out the blossom, which he accepted. Her sari was silken pink and gold embellishments, and the gold highlights glinted in the sun as she moved.

"What is this for?" he asked the child, holding the blossom in his trunk.

"It is so that you remember me," the girl replied.

Siam turned his head so that he could look closely at the child's face.

Her dark eyes sparkled in the diffused sunlight and she smiled at him.

"Are you the goddess?" he asked.

The little girl laughed an oddly familiar laugh.

"Silly Siam," she said. "I am Kalifa the Second."

Siam awakened from his dream with a start and rushed to the metal door, pressing his trunk to its cold, firm surface.

"Kalifa!" he shouted, addressing her familiarly.

Toni the Third, awakened by the sudden outburst, joined him at the door.

"What is the matter?" she asked.

"Kalifa!" shouted Siam, ignoring the matriarch.

The other elephants, confused by the commotion that had awakened them, gathered around.

"Siam," asked Taku the Second, "what's the matter?"

Siam turned from the door to face the herd, his expression blank.

"I had a dream about Kalifa the Second," he muttered.

"It was only a dream," replied Taku the Second. "Come back to bed."

Siam didn't argue. What could he do?

The next morning the herd learned that Kalifa the Second, overcome with fever from the infection in her foot, had died the night before. Siam took this news the hardest of any of the herd and refused to eat. Instead, he stood beside the familiar tree and watched the humans as they trekked past the elephant house. Concerned for his well-being, Toni the Third and Taku the Second approached him.

"Siam," said Taku the Second, touching her trunk to the side of his face, "you must eat. We are all worried about you."

Siam didn't look at the females.

"I'm fine," he said.

"You're not fine," replied Taku the Second. "If you don't eat you will die."

He turned to the females, his eyes filled with angry tears.

"We're all going to die," he snapped. "Isn't that the only reason we were brought here…to die?"

"Siam," pressed Taku the Second, "Kalifa the Second's death was an accident."

"And what of Carl, Mampe, Mary and Orje...and all of the others?" he yelled. "Were they all accidents, too?"

"It was their time," replied Toni the Second. "The goddess takes us when our time is up."

Siam felt in no position to argue the finer points of religion and so turned back to the tree without another word.

***

Slowly Siam's spirits improved and he began to eat once more, though his appetite was clearly not what it once had been. And, even though he seemed to be coping with Kalifa the Second's death and was at least speaking to the rest of the herd, much of his time was spent standing silently beside the tree, silently observing the passing humans, their numbers increased, according to zoo rumor, because of a visiting Panda from China.

Many times since the death of Kalifa the Second he closed his eyes and pictured the little girl in his dream, and this comforted him. One afternoon, in the third month, as he was standing beside his tree, as usual, he was surprised by a familiar voice.

"Siam? Is that you, old man?"

Siam raised his head without turning. He knew the voice, he was certain. He turned and, standing next to Toni the Third, was his childhood friend, Wastl. Siam hesitated a moment and then rushed toward the bull. The two mock sparred for a moment and then twined their trunks in a warm embrace.

Siam looked at Wastl, who he hadn't seen since the zoo in Munich. He had certainly grown and appeared healthy.

∙∙∙

"What are you doing here?" asked Siam, confounded. How was it that his childhood playmate had ended up here without his knowledge?

He had heard mention among the herd that an elephant had arrived but, in his state of mind, had largely ignored them.

"I go where they send me," replied Wastl.

"But, what of your mother, Cora, and your father, Boy?" asked Siam.

"Mother is well," replied Wastl. "She is caring for my brother, Seppl, and helping in the care of my sister, Stasi."

Siam explained that he had heard of the elephant births from the migrating crows.

"And Boy?" he pressed.

"My father is dead," replied Wastl. "He went crazy and broke off his tusks trying to escape."

Siam was shocked by the news and found it inconceivable that the proud Boy could be dead.

"The humans shot him," continued Wastl, "had to, I suppose. But," he said, smiling, "**at least the old man managed to father another baby before he died.**"

"With Cora, **right?**" asked Siam.

"No," replied Wastl, "with Mini. **Stasi is my half-sister.**"

"How wonderful," said Toni the Third, who had joined them, "but it's too bad about Boy."

"Anyway," said Siam, "you're here now. I never thought that I would see you again."

"I knew," said Wastl, "as soon as I saw the lorry...like the one they took you away in, I knew that I was coming to be with you."

Siam and Wastl talked late into the evening, catching up on all they had missed in the last six years. Siam told Wastl about the recent loss of Kalifa the Second and cursed the humans for placing the spikes at the bottom of the moat.

"They must have a good reason for putting them there," replied Wastl. Or else they wouldn't be there. The humans are an intelligent lot."

Siam was surprised at Wastl's indifference.

"And what about the metal rod?" he asked. "Is that necessary, too?"

"Like I said," replied Wastl, laughing. "The humans are an intelligent lot...everything they do has a purpose."

"Like bringing you here," asked Siam, "taking you from your mother and siblings?"

"As I said," replied Wastl, "I go where they send me and do my best to keep out of trouble. That way everything will be okay."

Siam couldn't help but be reminded of the day he was taken from his own mother and then it dawned on him: Wastl had been born in captivity. Life among the humans was all he had ever known. Like poor Kalifa the Second, he had never experienced life in the wild. With this realization, he decided to drop the matter altogether, just happy to have his old friend back by his side. Still, this attitude of blindly accepting all that the humans did troubled Siam. Perhaps, he secretly hoped, he could make Wastl change his opinion over time. Until then he would be patient.

Summer quickly came and monotony returned to the elephant house. Happy that his friend was with him once again, Siam didn't mind the routine but vowed to be more diligent in his watch over the herd. Never again would he allow what had happened to Kalifa the Second happen to any of the others. The rest of the herd stood resolutely behind him in this pledge, all promising to watch out for one another. Near the end of the summer, however, news reached the elephant house that made no sense: the humans, or so the rumors went, had begun a war against their human neighbors to the east. According to the apes, who were intelligent enough but whose word was often questioned by the other animals, their human captors were bombing cities in the east, among them Warsaw. Taku the Second, who had only left that city a year earlier, worried over her former herd confined in the zoo there. Siam did his best to reassure her.

"I'm sure your friends are fine," he said. "Besides, the apes sometimes embellish their gossip to make themselves look more human."

"Do you really think so?" she asked, clearly shaken.

"I know so," replied Siam. "Why would humans harm elephants in a zoo?"

But the truth of the matter was that he wasn't sure. Secretly, he wondered if this wasn't the incredibly stupid mistake that would lead to a shortage of food or, worse, their demise, as Mary had suggested years earlier.

When the crows returned in the fall they were oddly quiet about what they had seen in the east. Yach, who had an injured leg, spoke of "gigantic metal birds" but seemed interested in talking of anything else. When pressed for news of the Warsaw zoo, all he had to say were two words.

■■■

"Very bad," he squawked, shaking his head, "Very, very bad!"

His companion, Skeech, was even less talkative, his nerves obviously rattled by what he had seen.

"But, what about the elephants?" pressed Taku the Second, "Did you see any elephants?"

"No," screamed Yach, "no elephants!"

He and Skeech took flight, leaving the bewildered elephants behind.

Chapter Ten

1940

The apprehension with which Siam viewed the war in the east quickly proved to have been needless. Zoo gossip suggested quick victory for the armies of their captors and the happy faces of the humans visiting the zoo seemed to bolster these claims. In fact, within a little over a month after the beginning of hostilities, victory was declared by their human captors. Although Taku the Second worried about her former herd in Warsaw, the attitude among the elephants was one of relief. Grateful that they had suffered no setbacks as a result, the herd spent an uneventful winter with plenty of food and in general good health.

By the time spring came it brought with it new arrivals to the zoo. These arrivals, they soon learned were once housed in the zoo in Warsaw, and Taku the Second searched in vain for any of her elephant friends among them. Sadly, none appeared and word filtered back to the elephant house that the zoo in Warsaw had been destroyed by the humans, causing a great deal of deaths among the animals. As for the Warsaw elephants, nobody seemed to know their fate. Siam did his best to console Taku the Second, although he was concealing his own doubts. If the humans would destroy a zoo what made him so sure that they cared enough to spare the elephants? Nevertheless, he put on a brave face.

"I'm sure they are fine," he said, pressing his body against Taku the Second's.

"But how do you know?" she asked.

"I don't," replied Siam, "but, look, they brought other animals here. Maybe the elephants have been taken to other zoos."

"The zoo in Warsaw must have been an awful place," interjected Wastl. "Why else would the humans destroy it?"

"But it wasn't an awful place," grumbled Taku the Second. "The care I received there was just as good as the care I receive here."

Silenced, Wastl walked to the far end of the courtyard.

"Whatever the case," said Siam, in an attempt to calm his mate, "at least some of the animals have been moved to the safety of this zoo. We can only pray to the goddess that the elephants were moved to the safety of other zoos."

"He's right," said Toni the Third. "Try not to worry, dear."

"Listen," said Siam, "the zoo is good for gossip. Eventually, one of the new animals will talk about what happened and the news will reach us. For now all that matters is that we are safe."

Taku the Second nodded. Of course Siam was right.

***

One afternoon, as he stood watch over the grounds next to his tree, Siam spied a familiar face on the other side of the moat. Although he was much thinner and was without his beard, there was no mistaking the kindly old man. Siam approached the edge of the moat and, as he had done for the old human so many times before, lifted his foot in greeting. The old man smiled a faint smile, which accentuated the long lines on his face, but Siam could sense that he was very sad. On the breast of his overcoat was a bit of yellow cloth in the shape of a star. Siam could barely make out the word in the middle of the cloth, printed in black: *Jude*.

The word meant nothing to the elephant, although he wondered why the old man had suddenly reappeared wearing it. Siam trumpeted loudly, but the glee that the old man once got from watching the elephants was clearly gone. In response to Siam's theatrics, the old man turned out empty pockets to show that he had no peanuts. Then, with a feeble wave of his hand, he turned to go, tears staining his wrinkled cheeks.

Siam watched the old man until he vanished from sight and returned to his tree, deep in thought.

"Was that the human you told me about?"

Siam turned to face Taku the Second, who had joined his side.

"Yes," he replied, "but he seemed so different…so sad. And did you see that thing on his chest?"

"The star?" asked Taku the Second. "Yes, I saw it. What of it?"

Siam hesitated.

"I don't know," he finally replied. "It just seems odd that he was marked with that star, when he never wore it here before."

Taku the Second didn't know how to respond. Instead, she leaned on her mate to comfort him and they stood beside the tree late into the afternoon.

***

At the beginning of the fifth month, the inconceivable news that the armies of their captors had invaded their human neighbors to the west reached the zoo. This time Siam was convinced that the apes were lying. What kind of people would commit so many acts of aggression? But, when an elephant arrived in the middle of the month from the zoo in Cologne, she confirmed the rumors. The elephant, a wild-born African called Topsi, had known Tembo when they were at the Cologne zoo together. Topsi greeted Tembo but was obviously shaken by her experience. She spoke of "large metal birds," much as the ones Yach had described, that had dropped exploding eggs onto the city. Siam wrinkled his brow. Who had ever heard of exploding eggs? Wastl echoed his sentiments, accusing the poor elephant of being confused.

"No," she replied her eyes wide, "they came on the twelfth day of the month, and the noise was so loud that I thought I would never hear again."

"You're safe now," replied Toni the Second, "no exploding eggs have ever rained down on this zoo." The notion of exploding eggs struck Toni the Second, too, as wildly absurd but who was she to question the word of another elephant?

"She's right," agreed Tembo, who gently stroked her friend's head in an attempt to comfort her. "You are safe here."

Siam joined Wastl at the far end of the courtyard, where he had retreated in the face of the new elephant's rebuke.

"Exploding eggs?" he whispered to Siam as he approached.

"I know," replied Siam. "It sounds crazy, but **elephants do not lie. Perhaps she is confused by what she saw.**"

"Obviously," said Wastl.

"There were no exploding eggs in the jungle," commented Siam. "Sometimes I think that we would all be better off back in our homelands."

"This is my homeland," replied Wastl. "Can you imagine me roaming around some jungle?"

Wastl shuddered for effect and Siam laughed.

"I would be eaten by a tiger before I took my first step," continued Wastl. "And I certainly don't know how to forage for food."

"Still," replied Siam, "fending off tigers **has to be** better than exploding eggs."

Wastl could offer no argument to this last statement and silently nodded his head.

***

Spring turned to summer and, although Topsi seemed to have recovered from her experience at the Cologne zoo, Siam regularly caught her staring into the sky as if anticipating the return of the metal birds. The habit was disconcerting to the other elephants, almost hypnotic in fact, and Siam found himself scanning the horizon more than once. Wastl, of course, would have none of this.

"See any giant birds yet, old man?" he asked one afternoon in late August.

Siam turned, his face flushed red.

"I...I was looking for the crows," he stammered.

"It's a little early for the crows, isn't it?" teased Wastl.

But that evening, after the elephants had been herded into the elephant house for the night and the entire zoo seemed to be doing its best to sleep in the sweltering heat, Siam was awakened by a howling sound that he had never heard. The howling, which echoed across the zoo grounds, perhaps the entire city, seemed to emanate from all four directions at once. Siam lifted his right foot from the ground and fanned his ears in an attempt to discern the source of the noise, but Topsi already knew.

"The metal birds are coming!!!"

Her terrified shrieks almost seemed to drown out the howling but then a new sound pierced the night sky: the overhead drone of perhaps thousands upon thousands of bees. To an elephant, the tiny bee, made strong within a swarm is most terrifying. Even a tiger cannot inflict as much pain on a healthy adult as a swarm of bees, who can sting eye and ear and trunk. Siam turned to Topsi.

"What should we do?" he asked as the droning became louder.

"What can we do?" she sobbed. Tembo cowered next to her, looking nervously at the vaulted ceiling of the elephant house. Aida and Jenny the Second pressed their bodies together, creating a hiding place for the baby, Indra, between them. Lindi and Birma, scared out of their wits, clung to each other in the corner. Only Toni the Third, Taku the Second and Wastl joined Siam at the barred gate to stare into the darkness.

Suddenly, shafts of light pierced the night sky, seemingly reaching up to catch the metal birds. Siam wished that he could see the flying monsters but the darkness prevented this.

"Where are they?" yelled Wastl over the din.

Siam was about to reply that he couldn't see them when the first explosion shook the ground. Stunned, with a ringing in his ears that nearly deafened him, Siam staggered back from the opening of the elephant house. One of the females screamed. Another explosion and then another and another and then, suddenly, all was quiet. After a moment the strange howling that had preceded the attack filled the air. Siam turned to the gathered herd, thankful that none of them had been injured.

"Topsi," he said, "I'm sorry we doubted you."

"Me, too," said Wastl, joining Siam.

But the poor addled female didn't seem to hear them. With wide eyes, she addressed Toni the Third.

"You said that they never came here!"

"They never did," replied Toni the Third, "not until tonight."

Topsi looked at Toni the Third for a moment and then directed her gaze very slowly to each elephant, one at a time as if to say "I told you so." The herd was silent, save for the baby, Indra, who had begun feeding at her mother's teats. When nobody questioned her further, Topsi walked to the barred gate and looked out into the darkness.

"They will come again," she said.

None of the herd dared question this pronouncement, and soon the zoo was again quiet.

***

Perhaps prompted by the raid, and the next five that followed throughout the end of the summer and into the fall, the humans began work on a monster structure just outside the walls of the zoo to the north. It was the tenth month, and the leaves on the trees had once again turned yellow, orange and red and, for the most part, obscured the work being done but the elephants, Siam in particular, observed the construction with great interest. Huge cranes hauled copious amounts of materials as the structure grew taller and taller, blotting out the view of the nearby park.

"What do you suppose they are building?" asked Wastl, who had joined Siam to watch the workers.

"I have no idea," he admitted. "I hope it is to stop the metal birds."

Wastl agreed. The sooner the metal birds were gone the sooner life could return to normal. The herd, indeed the entire zoo, was exhausted with worry, never knowing when the attackers would return, always under the cover of darkness and making sleep nearly impossible. Siam turned to his old friend.

"Do you suppose the birds come as revenge for the war in the west?"

Wastl laughed, but it was a gruff, sarcastic laugh.

"How should I know?" he asked. "I mind my own business in order to keep out of trouble."

Siam regarded him for a moment, his eyes searching for a hint of the truth in his friend's face. If Wastl was frightened, he certainly didn't show it. Siam turned hi attention back to the construction.

"I suppose you're right," he said.

***

The following month, Topsi was taken away once again. This time, Siam noted that the lorry had the words "*Zoo Vienna*" written on the side, and he hoped that, wherever Vienna was, that there would be no more metal birds or exploding eggs. The herd wished the poor, frightened female a safe trip. Tembo, her old friend from the Cologne zoo, embraced her.

"It was nice while it lasted," she said. "Maybe I'll be moved again and, who knows, maybe see you at a new zoo."

As the lorry pulled away, Topsi managed to snake her trunk through an opening in the crate, waving a farewell to the herd.

Chapter Eleven

1941

The zoo enjoyed a quiet, if cold, winter. Although there were no further attacks from the air, the humans continued their feverish task of completing the mammoth structure outside the walls of the zoo. By the time the first leaves began to appear on the trees the monstrosity loomed high above the zoo, casting a long shadow over the ground and blotting out the view of the nearby park. To Siam, there was something unnatural about the structure, not just because of the enormity of its proportions, but its gray, concrete surface was hideous compared to the ancient trees it now hid from view. By the fourth month, construction completed, large, long-barreled objects were hauled to the top of the structure, objects not unlike the weapons that the humans had used to kill Siam's family, only much, much larger.

"No good will come of that thing," he commented to Taku the Second, "no good at all."

Taku the Second twined her trunk with Siam's, searching for a reply. Siam could sense that his mate had no opinion and he pressed his body against hers.

"No matter," he said. "If they stop the air attacks, then I suppose they will have proven useful."

"I don't like it either," said Toni the Third, who had joined them at the edge of the moat.

Siam regarded the matriarch for a moment. They had known each other since he had been a youth at the Munich zoo, and he suddenly felt a wave of affection for the older female. In fact, he suddenly realized that, had it not been for Toni the Third, the sudden death of Mary might have been his undoing. Maybe even the undoing of the entire herd. The matriarch suddenly became aware that Siam was staring at her.

"What?" she asked, a smile on her lips.

"Nothing," he replied after a moment, "everything."

"I just think it looks ugly," continued Toni the Third, gesturing at the new edifice looming on the horizon.

"So do I," agreed Taku the Second. "I preferred the trees to that thing."

Laughter in the far part of the courtyard caused the trio to turn and Siam laughed, too, when he heard Wastl, bragging about his warrior lineage to the other females.

"Just like his father," said Siam.

Toni the Third couldn't help but agree.

***

Spring passed quietly and more animals arrived at the zoo, from far way places with names like Rotterdam, Paris and Brussels. With them, they brought stories similar to the ones that came out of Warsaw, stories of explosions, fire and destruction. And, as with Warsaw, no elephants came as refugees from these new far away places, a development which Siam viewed as a bad omen. Again, the only arrivals were lions, tigers, horses and zebras. Perhaps elephants were simply too big, too slow moving to escape the exploding eggs. And, Siam reasoned, if this was the case then what chance did their own herd have the next time an attack was launched on their city? As usual, Wastl had an argument for this reasoning.

"They don't move the elephants because we are too big," he said, laughing off his friend's concerns. "The elephants from those zoos are still there, safe and sound."

"How do you know that?" asked Siam. Wastl may have been a very old friend, but his unwillingness to believe that the humans were capable of doing anything bad was beginning to get on his nerves.

"The humans are far too efficient to kill animals," replied Wastl. "You see how well we are cared for. Why would they harm us?"

"You don't know what you're talking about," said Siam, weary of the conversation. He might as well have been talking to a sparrow.

In fact, the herd was evenly divided in their opinion of the situation. While none of them relished the thought of more air attacks, their opinion of their human captors was varied. Lindi and Birma agreed more or less with Wastl, believing the humans incapable of intentionally harming an elephant, at least in a zoo. Aida and Jenny the Second, however, were far more apt to agree with Siam's contention that the humans were capable of anything. Siam guessed that their apprehension most probably stemmed from their concern over the safety of the baby, Indra, and Aida certainly had cause for caution after the death her own baby, Orje. Taku the Second, too, supported Siam, although he wasn't sure if she merely did so out of a sense of loyalty for her mate. Toni the Third wisely maintained a diplomatic air on the whole subject of the humans. As matriarch she had a responsibility for the well-being of the herd as a whole, so her attitude made some sense to Siam, but he secretly suspected that she took his side.

***

The summer was blessedly quiet, and human visitors flocked to the zoo, many in the green, blue or white uniforms of soldiers. As with the campaign in the east, the humans had enjoyed a quick victory against their human enemies to the west, yet they remained dressed as soldiers, as if in anticipation of further military actions in the future. Nevertheless, the humans who visited the zoo seemed in good spirits. And why shouldn't they, when their armies had scored so many victories against their enemies? Siam hated to admit it, but it was beginning to look as if Wastl had been correct in his assessment of the humans. After all, the zoo hadn't seen an attack since the previous autumn and there was no sign of a food shortage. In fact, the quantity of food had seemed to increase in the months since the most recent victory, a fact that Wastl was quick to point out to all who would listen. But, news that reached the elephant house near the end of the sixth month, on the occasion of the summer solstice, that the humans had launched another attack on the east, renewed Siam's feelings that something was terribly wrong.

"Why another war?" he asked Taku the Second. "What do the humans have to gain through so much aggression?"

Taku the Second tossed dirt onto her back in order to cool down before replying.

"Humans are brutal," she replied.

Her bluntness shocked Siam, who had never heard his mate speak so frankly, particularly regarding their human captors. He looked at her with astonishment.

"What do you mean?" he asked.

"You asked my opinion," she replied, "that is my opinion."

Siam laughed.

"It's just that I've never heard you speak this way."

Taku the Second looked at him, her face serious.

"After I was taken from my family," she said, her voice low, "I vowed never to speak of it again."

"Was it bad?" asked Siam.

"I thought that if I didn't do as I was told, that I **would end up like my** family…"

Taku the Second's voice trailed off, caught on the words.

"I lost my family, too," replied Siam. He touched Taku the Second's face with the tip of his trunk. "I'm sorry, you never told me."

"As I said," replied the female, "I vowed never to speak of it again, and I haven't until now. You understand me," she continued, "because you suffered the same injustice. But Wastl has never been in that position. He can never fully understand, so you must be patient with him."

Siam sighed, expelling a huge burst of air into the dust.

"You're right," he said, staring ahead.

"If something happens, we must stay together," said Taku the Second, "promise me."

Siam found his mate's trunk with his own.

"I promise," he whispered, "I will never let anything happen to you."

***

The summer died a slow and brilliantly colorful death, and news of victories in the east slowed as the weather became cooler. Nevertheless, the humans remained happy, even when soldiers appeared at the zoo covered in bandages or confined to rolling chairs, pushed by women in white.

In November the crows came, too and, for the second visit in a row, Yach was in bad spirits. His companion, Skeech, he explained, had been killed when the humans invaded their summering grounds in Russia. His new companion, a crow named Goff, seemed terrified by everything and jumped from the ground to the roof of the elephant house at the slightest sound.

"Too much boom," explained Yach.

Siam offered his sincere apologies to Yach, concerning the loss of Skeech and the old crow looked at Siam, exhaustion on his face.

"Humans bad," he squawked. "They destroy everything."

Siam replied that he was inclined to agree, that he feared they were all in grave danger, a notion that Yach found impossible to contradict. He passed on the news that Topsi, who had been sent to Vienna, was now at the Munich zoo. He wished the elephants well and flew off, Goff by his side, and disappeared into the trees of the nearby park. As he passed the monolithic structure outside zoo grounds he showed his distaste by squawking at it.

***

Two nights later the zoo was once again awakened by the howling sound and the drone of the approaching attackers. The elephants rushed to the gate that separated them from the courtyard and peered into the darkness. The droning overhead was louder than the previous raids and Siam watched as shafts of light, emanating from the top of the giant structure, shot suddenly into the dark skies. Jenny the Second was the only elephant that remained at the back of the elephant house, sheltering her baby, Indra, from the coming explosions.

"Get away from the gate!" she screamed at the other elephants.

Aida, Lindi, Tembo and Birma quickly joined her, terror on their faces. Only Siam, Taku the Second, Toni the Third and Wastl remained standing at the gate.

"Girls," implored Jenny the Second, "please. You're making me nervous. Let the silly males stand there if they want, but…"

She was cut off by the sound of the first explosion, which was muffled and far away. The second, third and fourth explosions were louder and in quick succession. Afraid and suddenly aware that she was behaving badly as matriarch, Toni the Third quickly joined the other females. Taku the Second turned to join them but stopped.

"Siam," she said, "Jenny the Second is right. Please come away from the gate before you're killed."

Siam hesitated for a moment, his heart pounding in his chest. As the next explosions rocked the ground, seemingly closer, however, he joined the females at the back of the building.

"Wastl," Taku the Second yelled over the tumult, "Get back here with us!"

But the young male wasn't listening. Instead, he remained where he stood, his eyes wide and his face illuminated by the blasts, excited by the action around them. He watched as fire belched from the top of the giant building just outside the walls of the zoo. Each time fire shot into the sky there was a loud retort, which reverberated, non-stop through the chilly air.

Siam gazed at the vaulted ceiling of the building. Dust rained down upon them each time the earth shook and the sparrows fluttered wildly among the beams, disturbed from their sleep. The drone in the sky was relentless, and Siam was sure that this raid was the biggest they had seen. When the sound of the attackers was gone the howling once again filled the air, punctuated now and then by smaller, more distant explosions. Relieved that they had once again emerged from the attack unscathed, Siam joined Wastl at the gate.

"It was amazing," Wastl said, breathless with exhilaration. "The big building was fighting back."

"What do you mean?" asked Siam. He looked at the building silhouetted against a clear sky.

"I don't know," stammered Wastl, "there was fire coming from the top of it...as if they were trying to hit the metal birds."

Siam considered this for a moment. If this was true then, perhaps, the building was a good thing, even if it did hide the trees of the nearby park from view. He turned to Wastl.

"I hope that they hit some of the birds," he said.

"They had to," replied Wastl. "It was amazing!"

***

Within days of the raid, more animals were removed from the zoo. The biggest blow came when Arra, a seventy-five year old parrot was taken away. Arra had been a fixture at the zoo for as long as any of the animals could remember and his departure made everyone wonder who would be next. Still, the majority of animals that were removed were smaller animals; birds, tropical snakes, deer and foxes. The elephants remained untouched by the evacuations.

As autumn turned to winter and winter into spring it became clear to the elephants that none of them were to be evacuated. This realization calmed Siam, who was grateful that, at least, they would all remain together. Although there were relatively few raids on the city that year, a total of nine, the zoo's inhabitants remained on edge, somewhere on a thin line between that of the insane and of the sleepwalker. And, as if the elephants needed any reminders of the realities of the stupid, human war, wounded soldiers continued to stream into the zoo at an alarming rate. As autumn once again returned to the zoo, Siam was cheered by a bit of good news. Rosa, the hippo, whose dwelling was adjacent to the elephant house, was pregnant. To have been reminded that life continued even among such destruction was a welcome diversion.

When Yach and Goff arrived the following month, however, they brought with them troubling news. The humans, they explained, had set up vast human zoos in the east. In these zoos, Yach explained, humans fenced in and killed other humans, burning their bodies until the air was thick with smoke and ash. Never, he concluded, had he seen such behavior from humans. Goff, who seemed to have regained his faculties since his last visit to the zoo, agreed.

"Bad, bad place," he said.

This news troubled Siam. If the humans were willing to put their own kind into zoos and burn them, what chance did the elephants have?

He thanked Yach for the news but, for once, decided to keep the story of human zoos to himself. There was no need, he decided, to frighten the already frightened females.

■■■

Chapter Twelve

1943

As the winter and the third full year of war drew to a close, the elephants emerged from the safety of the elephant house to welcome the spring. By the time the first spring flowers, crocuses, hyacinth and tulips, began to bloom and the air carried on it the scent of new life the attacks on the zoo began anew. It was, to the animals of the zoo, as if the metal birds, too, had emerged from hibernation to pick up where they had left off in the autumn. But, despite the air attacks over the winter, the war had been greatly in evidence by the throngs of wounded soldiers who visited the zoo and mirrored in the unhappy faces of all of the humans who came. It was during the second month of the year that news reached the zoo of the surrender of their captor's army in Russia. Siam had immediately assumed, as did most of the animals that this meant the end of the war but, to their utter amazement, it did not and the war raged on.

"How can they continue to fight when they've lost a whole army?" asked Siam. "It seems insane."

"Insanity to a human is clearly very different than what insanity means to an elephant," opined Toni the Third.

"Their army is vast," said Wastl. "They will fight on."

Siam wanted to ask his friend just how he knew that their army was vast, but he didn't press the matter. Most likely he had been listening to the sparrows.

"It seems senseless to me," said Siam. "Besides, we don't even know why the war was begun in the first place."

A general discussion broke out among the herd, Wastl suggesting that the war was caused because the humans had been attacked, Taku the Second suggesting that it was because the humans merely wanted to steal neighboring land and Toni the Third suggesting that it was all merely sport on the part of the humans. Siam was inclined to agree with Taku the Second, maybe even Toni the Third, but instead offered another opinion.

"Humans like to destroy," he said, "like they destroyed our families in the wild."

The herd fell silent. After a moment it was Wastl who spoke.

"That's nonsense," he said. "Look at how well we are treated here. If they wanted to have killed us they would have done so already."

"Like my mother?" snapped Siam, "or your father?"

∙∙

Wastl bristled at the mention of Boy.

"My father was out of his head," he replied. "The humans had no choice!"

"Your father was out of his head from years of imprisonment," countered Siam.

Wastl raised his tusks and took a step toward Siam. Toni the Second rushed between the males.

"Stop it!" she said.

The two males backed away in deference to the matriarch but eyed one another over her. Taku the Second stepped beside Siam.

"Come with me," she said.

Siam started to object but, seeing the serious look on his mate's face, followed her to the end of the courtyard, away from the other elephants.

■■■

"I'm sorry," he said, his head low.

"You can't let Wastl get to you like that," she said. "He's a foolish zoo-**born. He forgets that there is more to** life than fences and regular feedings."

"I know," replied Siam. "It won't happen again."

"Good," replied Taku the Second, "because I don't want my baby's father to be killed in some stupid scuffle."

It took a moment for the female's words to register but, when they did, Siam's face came alive. He looked at the **other females, who were standing a few feet away, smiling at the couple.**

"A baby?" he asked. "Are you sure? How **do you** know?"

Taku the Second laughed.

"Of course I am sure," she replied. "An elephant knows these things."

The females of the herd, who had been holding back just long enough for Taku the Second to break the news, now surrounded the pair and reached to touch them with their outstretched trunks. Only Wastl, his ego wounded, stood back. Siam, feeling suddenly remorseful, approached his friend.

"Wastl," he said, "I apologize for what I said. I was wrong to bring up Boy."

Wastl didn't look up from the ground for a moment, as he contemplated Siam's apology. When he finally raised his head Siam was relieved to see him smiling.

"Of course I forgive you, old man," he said. "Elephants cannot be enemies to one another."

Taku the Second joined the males and stoked Siam's face with her trunk.

"Congratulations on the news," said Wastl, addressing them both.

"Thank you," replied Siam. "It looks like I'm going to be a father!"

"A zoo-born baby," said Wastl. "Try not to be so hard on him."

"I'm hoping that his Uncle Wastl can help me with that," replied Siam.

As news of the pregnancy spread to other parts of the zoo, congratulations arrived. Rosa, the hippo, whose own baby was due that spring, was particularly pleased.

"She's got it lucky," commented Taku the Second, though not unkindly, "hippos only carry their young for eight months. I will carry my baby for nearly two years."

"The time will fly by," said Jenny the Second, whose sentiments were echoed by Aida.

"It will," she said, "and we will all be here to help you."

In fact, it was one night near the end of the fifth month when the hippo, Rosa, gave birth during an air attack. Her moans and obvious discomfort were nearly drowned out by the sounds of the explosions, although her companions, Olga and Zuzana, tried comforting her through the birth. By the time the attackers had departed she was the proud mother to a little male, who the humans dubbed Knautschke. Again, there was very little damage inflicted upon the zoo itself, the majority of the destruction limited to neighboring areas. The monolithic, fire spitting building, it seemed, was doing a good of job protecting the zoo and its inhabitants.

One morning, after a particularly heavy air attack, Siam and Taku the Second stood beside the tree listening to the baby hippo playing in its nearby pond. The air was thick with smoke and the elephants were tired from sleep deprivation, but the sounds of the baby hippo lifted their spirits.

"Soon we will have one of our own," sighed Taku the Second.

"A hippo?" joked Siam.

Taku the Second laughed.

"That would be something," she said.

Siam looked at the baby elephant, Indra, playing nearby. In her trunk she held a clump of grass and carried it in front of her as if she was holding a precious treasure.

"I wish our baby could be born in the wild," he said after a moment.

He kept his voice low, not wanting Wastl to overhear.

"As do I," replied Taku the Second. "But at least we know that here our baby will always be fed and receive medical attention."

"Or be killed in a raid," said **Siam**.

Taku the Second embraced Siam, despite his dark mood.

"Remember what you promised me," she said, "that we will always stay together."

"I promise," replied Siam, his mood lightening.

***

When summer arrived the elephants learned that Tembo was to be evacuated from the zoo. The words *Zoo Munich* were written in chalk on the side of the lorry that waited outside the elephant house and she seemed sad to leave, although both

Lindi and Birma confessed that they were jealous, if only to be away from the air attacks.

"Who knows?" said Toni the Third. "Perhaps you will catch up with Topsi again."

"That would be nice," she agreed. "The poor thing would probably enjoy seeing a familiar face."

She bade the herd goodbye and was prodded into the lorry. As it drove away she called to her friends.

"I hope to see you all again soon!" she cried. "May the goddess keep you safe!"

And then the lorry was gone, disappearing through the gate and out of sight.

Once it was quiet again, Wastl spoke.

"Why would they bring me here and send Tembo there?" he asked. "It doesn't make any sense."

Siam was tempted to tease Wastl for doubting his "all knowing" humans, but refrained. He had given his word to Taku the Second that he would make a better effort to maintain peace and he was determined to keep his word. Besides, Wastl had recently grown aggressive, not because of the raids but because, Siam suspected, he was nearing musth. Knowing all too well the effects of musth on the male psyche, Siam vowed to be extra careful in his dealings with the younger male. To do otherwise could endanger the entire herd and, with a pregnant cow and a baby present, the last thing he wanted to see was a raging bull amongst them.

By the time the leaves on the trees had begun to change color, Siam's suspicions were confirmed. Urine trickled down Wastl's hind legs and powerful smelling secretions stained his face. When the crows arrived in November Wastl had become nearly uncontrollable and the rest of the herd maintained a safe distance from the hormone addled bull. Thankfully, Yach arrived in better spirits and brought news that Siam hoped would soon mean the end of the war. The humans, Yach explained, were losing battles not only in the east, but also in the west and south.

"That's wonderful news," whispered Siam. "If they continue to retreat, surely that will mean the end of the attacks on the city."

"I hope," agreed Yach. Goff, perched nearby, squawked in agreement.

Unfortunately, Wastl was eavesdropping.

"Why do you waste your time talking to crows?" he bellowed. He hurled a bit of uneaten melon at the crows, who squawked loudly and flew to Siam's back for safety.

Yach narrowed his eyes at the offending bull.

"Ach," he said, "he has the stink!"

Wastl charged toward them but they flew to the safety of the roof of the elephant house.

"Go away!" he yelled at them.

"Oh, shut up!" yelled Yach. He turned back to Siam.

"Your female, Tembo, is well at the Munich zoo," he said. "But the one called Topsi was moved to the Breslau zoo."

"Thank you," replied Siam, saddened that the females had been separated once more.

Siam watched as the crows took to the air, no doubt headed for the safety of the nearby park. He turned and regarded Wastl for a moment.

"What are you looking at?" asked Wastl, his head aching.

Siam didn't bother to answer. He knew that nothing he could possibly have said would be taken well. He was sorry for Wastl but the news from the crows had lifted his spirits. With any luck, the armies would soon surrender and fighting would stop. Then, he hoped, peace would return to the zoo.

***

It wasn't long after the crow's visit that Wastl attacked Toni the Third. As they had done when Siam had first suffered the effects of musth, the humans decided that it would be best to quarantine him in the separate cage used for that purpose. Unfortunately, the humans decided to place Siam in isolation, as well. Siam protested that he was not suffering musth but, as he had learned so often before, there was no arguing with the man and his iron rod and he was prodded into the isolation cell with Wastl. Once the humans had gone and the two males were locked away from the females, Taku the Second joined Siam at the bars that separated them.

"I'm sorry, Siam," she said, poking her limber trunk through the bars and finding his. "You will be out before you know it."

"But I'm not suffering musth," he argued. "I should be with you…especially if the attacks come."

"We will be sleeping on the other side of the wall," she said, "and at least we can talk through this gate."

Siam sighed. She was right, of course, but he already missed sleeping next to her and said as much.

"Look at it this way," she whispered, "at least you can keep Wastl company until he gets better. You have been through musth, you know how it feels."

Siam considered this for a moment but, before he could reply, Wastl grumbled from behind.

"I didn't ask for his damned company!"

Siam rolled his eyes at Taku the Second and she squeezed his trunk in a way that said to him, "be strong." He looked at Wastl and was suddenly filled with a feeling of filial comradeship. Musth was difficult, Siam knew, and he would do what he could to help his friend.

That night, after all of the females were herded into the larger chamber within the elephant house, Siam heard Taku the

Second's voice gently whispering his name. He walked to the end of the isolation chamber and found her trunk, jutting out of the opposite chamber in the darkness. He twined his trunk in hers and held it for a moment. Although he couldn't see her, he could feel his mate through the thick wall.

"Goodnight," she said.

"Goodnight," he repeated.

He was awakened a few hours later by the howling sound, which echoed off of the zoo's walls. The overhead drone of the metal birds could be heard as well as the thump of the guns atop the concrete structure as they attempted to repel the invaders. He turned to find Wastl staring up at the sky through the barred gate. Siam rushed to the opposite end of the chamber and reached around the corner, into the female's chamber.

"Taku the Second!" he called.

He felt her trunk quickly grasp his and she held on tight. He cursed his luck, being separated from her during a raid. Suddenly, the sound of explosions began to reverberate in the air around them, shaking the ground and causing dust to rain down from the rafters. As the explosions grew nearer Siam could feel the walls of the elephant house moving, and he realized that neither of them should have been standing at the fence. He wrestled his trunk from her grip.

"Get away from the fence," he yelled. "Go stand with the other females!"

"I don't want to leave you!" replied Taku the Second, her voice trembling.

The sound of explosions drew nearer and Siam had difficulty hearing over the din.

"I'll be right here!" he replied. "If we stay by the open bars we could be killed, now go!"

Toni the Third called to her from among the huddled, frightened females.

"Taku the Second!" she cried. "Get over here in the corner with us! Get away from the opening!"

Taku the Second hesitated a moment, finally realizing that Siam and the matriarch were right. Grudgingly, she joined the rest of the females, who were huddled at the back of the chamber, protecting the baby, Indra, with their bodies. Siam turned and called to Wastl.

"Get away from the gate!" he yelled.

"Look at this!" replied Wastl, his eyes wide.

Siam rushed to Wastl's side and stopped in his tracks. The reptile house, such a large and imposing structure, was aflame, its roof blasted open. Flames licked through broken windows and human figures could be seen darting in and out of the doomed structure. Siam was just about to suggest to Wastl that they retreat to the middle of the room when light as bright as the sun filled the elephant house he was knocked to his knees by an explosion more powerful than he had ever felt. Bricks and plaster rained down on the two males and when Siam pulled himself up from the ground he was sure that he was deaf; although he could see explosions in the distance, he no longer heard them. His eyes burned with dust and smoke and he looked up to see Wastl, standing in the courtyard, having escaped from a hole made in the wall by the force of the blast. Dead sparrows littered the floor of the chamber, apparently killed by the force of the explosion. Siam took care not to step on the dead birds and made his way through the hole and walked out into the courtyard in a daze. He was shocked to see numerous animal enclosures engulfed in flames. Then he remembered Taku the Second.

He slowly turned around to face the elephant house, and was horrified to see that it was gone, a smoldering heap of ruins. Only the adjacent isolation chamber where he and Wastl were being kept had been spared. Gasping for breath in the thick, curling smoke, Siam ran to where the females had been but was forced back by the intense heat.

"Taku the Second!" he screamed. "Taku the Second!"

He fell back, sickened by the realization that all of the females were dead. Aida, Jenny the Second, her baby, Indra, Lindi, Birma, Toni the Third and Taku the Second, along with his unborn baby, all dead in one indiscriminate and horrible instant.

"Come on!" Wastl yelled.

The sound of his friend's voice made Siam realize that his hearing had returned, but it was as if he was hearing from deep under water. He turned and was surprised to see Wastl standing on the human side of the moat, which he had crossed thanks to a bridge created by a pile of rubble from the collapsed wall.

"Come on!" repeated Wastl. "You wanted to be free. This is our chance!"

Siam wanted to join Wastl but found that he couldn't move. It was as if his feet had been chained to a tree. He stood, unmoving, even as bits of tile were blown from neighboring roofs and bounced off of his tough skin.

After a moment Wastl turned to go, confused by his friend's inaction. Wastl didn't know where to go. All he knew was that he no longer relished the thought of having explosives dropped on him in the middle of the night. Perhaps, he thought, Siam had been right about captivity. Perhaps elephants were not meant to be kept in cages. Wastl passed a dead giraffe, its eyes still open. He stared at its long tongue, which lay gray and lifeless on the ground. A wolf, terrified and injured, ran past him and disappeared into some bushes. More explosions shook the ground and Wastl ran to his right, past a burning building. Inside, monkeys screamed their last breaths. A zebra, freed from its destroyed house, ran past, terrified, and a rhinoceros, mortally wounded, coughed blood onto the ground where it lay motionless.

Suddenly, Wastl saw an opening to the street and began running. As he approached it he realized that this was the famous elephant gate, its roof blasted off. He looked at the concrete elephants, which had once flanked the gate but were now lying on the ground, blown from their pedestals. Ignoring them, he rushed out onto the street, cutting his feet on broken glass and masonry. Lorries sat frozen where they had stopped, ablaze. The big building across the street, the one with all of the spires and colored windows, was burning, its walls crumbling slowly inward. Across the wide avenue he could see the large glass-roofed building ablaze, too. The small cars, the ones that carried the humans, sat frozen on their tracks. More explosions rocked the ground and Wastl stopped, surrounded by walls of fire, unsure where to go. It was as if Phi-ra had descended in anger.

Where could he go that was safe? He hesitantly turned and ran back into the zoo, the only safety he had ever known. Siam would tell him what to do, he was much wiser. As he passed the burning reptile house he saw that the ground in front of it was littered with dead and dying crocodiles. Blood poured from their noses and mouths. Suddenly, the zoo director appeared, carrying a long gun, which he pointed at the escaped bull.

It was not the loudest of the sounds that accosted Siam that night, and perhaps he only imagined that he had heard it, but the shot that felled Wastl changed Siam forever.

Chapter Thirteen

The next morning, the extent of the damage to the zoo was more obvious. Although thick smoke hung in the air like fog clinging to a jungle canopy, Siam could see, even through the obscured sunlight, that the zoo had been all but destroyed. The neighboring flamingo house was silent, the water surrounding it a mass of unmoving pink, dead flamingoes. Clearly, this was all the result of the "incredible act of stupidity" the elephants had feared the humans had been capable of all along.

As soon as the first light permitted him to do so, Siam forced himself to explore what remained of the elephant house. The portion of the building that had housed the females was practically flattened and the bars that had once covered the front of the structure were now bent backwards in a grotesque shape, so that the top, which had been connected to the roof, now touched the ground.

The only opening in the rubble that allowed Siam any sort of view inside the chamber was near the isolation chamber where he and Wastl had been sleeping. Here the roof had only partially collapsed and he peered inside, spotting only a lone trunk and foreleg poking from beneath the rubble. He sniffed the air and determined that the trunk belonged to poor Lindi. All else that he was able to smell over the smoke and dust was blood, lots and lots of blood. Lying alongside Lindi was another animal and it took Siam to realize that it was a rhinoceros, who had apparently escaped its own destroyed house only to be killed alongside the female elephants. He was jarred from his stupor by the sounds of gunshots and turned to see the humans killing more escaped animals. Terrified, he made his way back through the hole in the wall and into the isolation chamber. The dead sparrows that he had noticed the night before still littered the floor, their bodies cold and stiff. Gingerly, he began picking up the lifeless forms and placing them in a pile in the corner. He had considered them a bit of a nuisance in life but, in death, he realized that they were victims the same as every other creature in the zoo. Big tear drops exploded on the ground beneath him as he reverently moved each sparrow. When he was finally done with his task, he stood in the middle of the desolate chamber and waited, tears streaming down his cheeks. Siam didn't know why he was crying. Did he weep because he was frightened? Were his tears the tears of mourning? Or were they tears of anger? Anything seemed possible at that moment and so Siam stood, waiting.

Maybe now, he told himself, they would move him back to Munich, away from the attacks. At least there, he wouldn't be alone.

***

Sometime near the middle of the day (he couldn't be sure because the sun was still blotted out by the smoke in the air) the zoo director appeared at the elephant house, his expression grave. His face was unshaven, his hair a mess and he looked as if he hadn't slept in days. Even his normally vibrant blue eyes seemed to have lost their sparkle and black soot covered one cheek. He was accompanied by the man with the iron rod and two other men in white uniforms. The uniforms were a one-piece sort of garment and were covered in soot, too. With the uniforms they wore black boots and Siam regarded them as the zoo director spoke to the men in hushed tones, pointing here and there. The zoo director looked at Siam for a long moment, and the veins stood up on his forehead. Suddenly, he turned and was gone and the men in the white uniforms began to brick up the hole in the side of the isolation chamber. Siam watched them as they worked and offered them no resistance. Within hours, he was once again walled in and the two men disappeared.

Throughout the day, news of other deaths filtered back to Siam. Olga, one of the hippos, had been killed but the baby, Knautschke, was well as was his mother, Rosa. Two gorillas were dead, giraffes, zebras and virtually every creature in the aquarium and reptile house. The hippo, reptile, kangaroo, tiger and elephant houses are all badly damaged, many to the point of being irreparable. Late in the afternoon, a tiny spider monkey suddenly appeared outside Siam's chamber. He peered inside, as if uncertain whether or not he should enter. The sounds of human voices drawing near seemed to have made up his mind for him, however, and he scurried through the bars and into a dark corner of the cell. He looked terrified and looked from side to side each time he heard a loud noise; Siam could see that the hand on his right arm was badly burned, and the monkey, who introduced himself as Charlie, held the injured hand close to his body.

"Your people are dead, too?" asked Charlie, his voice tiny.

"Yes," replied Siam.

Charlie didn't say anything, just nodded his head, a sad, lost look on his tiny face.

"I saw your other male over there," he finally said, pointing with his uninjured hand. "He was lying next to a dead horn nose."

Siam sighed, suddenly realizing that Wastl was dead, as he had feared. Now he was truly alone.

Charlie went on to explain that the zoo director's residence was destroyed, too, a little tidbit that, for some reason made Siam happy. If the animals had to suffer on account of the human's stupid war, it only seemed fair that the humans suffer as well. Charlie agreed.

Later that evening, just as the sun set, the humans appeared at the cage with hay, fresh water and vegetables. When they spotted the monkey huddled in the corner, one of the men made as if to catch him. Charlie shrieked and scrambled onto Siam's back, unwilling to be captured. Siam lumbered toward the man, his trunk high and his ears wide and the man quickly exited the cage in terror. The man with the iron rod quickly appeared and sized up the situation. As he entered the cage, however, he was thrown to the ground with a single swipe of the elephant's trunk. He quickly stood and exited the cage. Once outside, he stared at Siam for a moment. He didn't appear angry. In fact, Siam sensed great sadness from the handler. He turned to his co-workers and barked an order and they quickly retreated. Once they had gone, Charlie scrambled down to the floor.

"Thank you," he said, still clutching his burnt hand.

"You are welcome to stay with me," said Siam. "There is plenty to eat and, as we are alone, I see no reason not to keep each other company."

Charlie considered this for a moment and then nodded his head.

"The next time they come," said Siam, as he ate hay and Charlie munched on a bit of melon, "climb onto my back, as you did, but then go to the rafters. There they will be unable to reach you even if they beat me."

Charlie looked up at the ceiling as if to take in what Siam was saying and then resumed his meal.

That night the attackers returned, awakening the unlikely pair from a fitful sleep. Terrified, Charlie scampered up Siam's trunk and stopped to rest just behind one of the elephant's ears, which he grasped tightly using his good hand. As noise of the explosions grew louder, Charlie's high-pitched screams were drowned out by the noises around them. He remained on Siam's head, shivering, well after quiet had returned to the zoo.

The next few days were hellish for the lone elephant. The dead females had begun to stink, despite the cooler temperatures and the attackers returned again night after night, setting the surrounding landscape alight. It was only the unexpected companionship of the little monkey that prevented Siam from going insane. Charlie, too, seemed grateful for his new friend, although his wounded hand clearly caused him pain. Each time the human handlers appeared with food, the little monkey did as Siam told him, first climbing up onto the elephant's back and then leaping onto the rafters above. This strategy seemed to work, for the humans went about their work, seemingly disinterested in the escaped monkey. It was clear from all that was going on around them that they had more urgent matters to attend to than one little simian.

It took the humans one week to remove the dead elephants from the destroyed enclosure. First, men in the white uniforms appeared carrying pickaxes, shovels and rope. They meticulously removed the rubble, placing it onto the backs of waiting Lorries. Once the debris was removed, however, the stench from the dead females became almost unbearable and the task of removing the mammoth creatures began in earnest. When workers appeared carrying, axes and saws to complete the task, Siam could not comprehend what was happening; it was the sounds of the saws cutting into the tough, festering flesh that jarred him from his stupor. It was as if he was reliving his capture all over again. Siam screamed in protest and raged against the bars of his cage, frightening not only the workers but also Charlie, who retreated to the safety of the rafters to avoid being trampled by the raging bull. The humans wore cloths tied around their necks to cover their mouths and noses, repulsed by the smells they encountered and each time they passed his cage, Siam pelted them with anything he could grasp, bits of fallen masonry, pebbles, and even dead sparrows. But when the Lorries appeared, the ones bearing the word "Rudnitz," and Siam spied pieces of the females being tossed unceremoniously onto the backs of them, he collapsed into a heap on the floor of his chamber, sobbing until he thought his heart would explode. Charlie leapt from his hiding place in the rafters and cautiously approached the broken bull. When he was certain that the elephant meant him no harm he inched up onto Siam's head and laid down, softly stroking the tough skin beneath him. Now and again Charlie would shriek at the humans but never moved from his position atop the wounded elephant.

It took the humans one week to remove the dead animals from the zoo. Each day Siam watched as the caravans departed the zoo, destined for the place he knew only by name, the machines packed with the lifeless forms of elephants, zebras, panthers, ostriches, seals and flamingoes, some intact some dismembered and burnt, a horrific, twisted menagerie. While the haphazard and broken piles of bodies lent an air of chaos to the scene, Siam recognized the actions of the humans for what they were: cold, calculated and maddeningly orderly. Was this how it was in the human zoos that Yach had told him about? As he watched, only two words came to mind:

Dog food.

■■■

Siam turned away from the perverted spectacle and looked for Charlie, who had been sneaking out of the cage in search of news of zoo survivors. Already, he had brought the news that along with the hippos, Zuzana, Rosa and her baby, Knautschke, five lions, including the nine month old cubs, Sultan and Bussy, the chimpanzee, Suse, the gorilla, Pongo, the rare stork, Abu, had all survived the bombing, along with bears, zebras, hartebeests, horses, foxes, hyenas, Tibetan cats and a lone baboon. There was even talk that evacuations would begin soon, in an effort to move the surviving animals out of harm's way. This news bolstered Siam for, if he was evacuated, perhaps the humans would send him to the Munich zoo where he could be reunited with Cora and Tembo. He was snapped from this fantasy by movement in the street in front of the destroyed elephant house. He looked and saw that it was Charlie making his way back, scampering along on all fours, his damaged hand curled into a little black fist. The monkey appeared to be in a hurry and, as he neared the cage, failed to see the humans just to his left lying in wait behind some bushes. Siam trumpeted a warning but it was too late. One of the humans tossed a net onto the little ape, trapping him. Charlie, lying helpless on the ground, screamed in protest and showed his teeth but the humans, who were wearing thick gloves, picked him up and carted him away. His screams echoed in the cold air long after Siam lost sight of him.

Siam lowered his head, the realization that he was once again alone filling him with dread.

***

As the zoo entered the twelfth month of the year the evacuations that Charlie had heard mentioned began in earnest. There had been no air attacks for well over a week and Siam surmised that this was on account of the gloomy weather. He also guessed that, in the absence of attacks from the sky, the humans had decided to take advantage of the lull by moving the remaining animals to safety. He watched from his chamber as birds, monkeys, zebras and horses filed past, headed for unknown destinations and, although he looked for him, didn't see Charlie amongst the evacuees.

As the month grew colder and snow blanketed the ground, Siam finally accepted the fact that he was not to be among the animals moved to other zoos. The two air attacks that came near the end of the month had little effect on the forlorn bull, nor did they do much damage to the zoo, their targets apparently to a neighboring district to the south. To Siam, the attacks were now nothing more than a diversion and, goddess willing, a possible release from his miserable existence.

■■■

Chapter Fourteen

1944

The first day of the New Year brought not only colder weather but also a nighttime attack from the sky. Siam stood passively in his chamber as the sound of explosions grew nearer, praying that the goddess would allow one of the exploding eggs to find him and end his misery. But he was spared that night just as he was spared when the attackers returned the following night and the night after that. The fourth night was inexplicably quiet but the attackers returned the next night, again sparing the zoo from harm. There were a total of nine attacks in the first month and Siam remained unscathed, but alone and angry, nevertheless. During the daytime he stood in the courtyard beside the familiar tree, waiting for the human visitors which no longer came. The music from the outdoor café had ceased, too. In the distance he could see the burned out shell of the aquarium and reptile house, its once white façade stained black around the blown out windows, but most of the evidence of the raids was concealed under a thin blanket of snow. He ignored the barren concrete slab where the elephant house had once stood, the lingering smells there were simply too much for the grief stricken elephant to bear. He no longer trusted his human keepers and lunged angrily if they tried to enter his chamber, even when they arrived bearing food and water. Why should he trust humans? He asked himself. It was humans who had caused all of the misery surrounding him; it was humans who cut off the water to the hippo house, causing Rosa's skin too peel and it was humans who took poor Charlie away. He hated them, food or no food, and would kill them if they ever entered his cage. Withdrawing further from the realities of the zoo, Siam stopped eating and began to lose weight. The atmosphere of gloom hung over the zoo, affecting every creature there. Like Siam, the gorilla, Pongo, refused his food and stared blankly at nothing, threatening anyone who neared his cage. The only animal who seemed oblivious to the deprivations thrust upon the zoo was the baby, Knautschke, who played as if nothing was wrong. Siam envied the little hippo's innocence and thought sadly of Taku the Second and his unborn baby.

News made its way to Siam, via zoo gossip, that human zoo workers were sneaking small animals out of the zoo in order to care for them in their homes. Several monkeys and Abu, the Stork, the gossip said, had all been secretly removed from the zoo in this way. Siam realized that his sheer size would make such an escape impossible, but hoped that Charlie was one of the monkeys that had been removed to safety. Unfortunately, nobody could confirm whether or not this was true.

■■

Another large raid came in the middle of the second month, further setting the nerves of the zoo's inhabitants on edge, but an even worse development came near the beginning of the third month, when the attackers appeared in the daylight. At first Siam couldn't believe what he was seeing, the small flying forms too high up for him to truly identify, but the sound they made was unmistakable. Long white trails followed them against the blue sky. The howling sound that preceded them echoed across the zoo as if to confirm the attacker's existence. Explosions rocked the city's sandy soil and great plumes of smoke arose to the west. Siam stood, mesmerized by the spectacle. The attackers streamed overhead, seemingly unopposed, until the towering building outside the zoo's walls came to life, its twin guns pumping round after round into the sky. Explosions erupted in the sky above and bits of metal rained down on the zoo. After a while, the attackers were gone, their sounds fading in the distance and leaving behind raging fires, the smoke that was born of the conflagration and the sounds of muffled, far away explosions. Siam trumpeted loudly at the sky, a protest that he had intended for the attackers but, as he considered the sky, which was darkened with smoke and ash, he realized that his protest was meant for more than the attackers.

The goddess had clearly deserted him. Clearly the god, Phi-ra, god of fire and destroyer of life was now in charge of the universe.

Siam raged at the sky, trumpeting and charging back and forth until he was out of breath. To hell with the goddess, he said. She had allowed him to be brought to this place, allowed his mother to be killed, allowed Taku the Second to be killed and hadn't even cared enough about him to allow Charlie to remain at his side. Siam's fury was so intense that even the baby, Knautschke, in his nearby pen grew quiet. Exhausted and hopeless, he went back inside his shelter and looked around as if searching for something. Frustrated by the sparse room, Siam began beating his trunk against the wall where he had last spoken to Taku the Second, the night of the raid that killed her. The sound of his trunk hitting the concrete was hollow and relentless and painful, but the sensation made him feel alive. Bits of plaster fell in response to the abuse, showering the mad elephant. His battered trunk left splotches of blood on the wall and, seeing this, he stopped, remembering the message he had encountered in the isolation chamber upon his arrival at the zoo. Using the tip of his battered and shivering trunk he wrote upon the wall in elephant script.

"I AM DA-RA!"

He stood back and admired his handiwork. It was the first thing in days, months even, that had made him smile. Unfortunately, his good mood was dampened by another air attack that night. Obviously, the goddess was punishing him for his sacrilege, and he ran into the courtyard, bellowing at the sky.

"What do you want of me?" he cried, his voice barely discernable over the raging battle around him. "Why are you allowing this to happen to us?"

Bombs exploded nearby but Siam remained in the courtyard, screaming, as bits of debris showered down upon him. He remained standing there until the attackers had finally gone.

Although Siam couldn't have known it, the tactic of daylight bombing alongside of the regular nighttime bombings was to be repeated all through the third month.

The last raid, somewhere near the end of the month, was limited to an area far from the zoo and was of little consequence to the zoo's inhabitants. Then, inexplicably, the bombings ceased altogether. Nearly out of his mind from lack of sleep and his refusal to eat, Siam had trouble comprehending that there were no attacks in the following days but, as spring slowly unfolded into summer, quiet once again descended upon the city. Human visitors once more appeared at the zoo, not in droves like the early days, but enough to make an impression on the otherwise distracted elephant. The humans who came were mostly women and children, although they too, now wore some type of uniform. The fatigue on the faces of these humans mirrored the fatigue that Siam felt and, for the first time in years, he felt camaraderie towards the humans. Not sympathy, however; it was the humans who had begun the war, had killed so many, so why should an animal feel sorry for those who had sown so much destruction? Still, Siam couldn't help but feel a strange sort of kinship with the sad, tired eyed humans who filed past the pathetic cages. And of the men who came to the zoo, Siam felt closeness, pity almost, for these men were either old or severely wounded. The men in uniform who appeared on the other side of the moat were a testament to the stupidity of war, their faces disfigured by fire, their limbs shorn off, and their legs useless. But the one thing that remained the same was the human's love of decorations. On the chests and around the necks of these pathetic cripples, these children of war were all manner of medals, colorful ribbons and decorations. Obviously there was merit in having had half of your face eaten away by fire. No, thought Siam, turning away from a human who was missing both hands, he would never understand humans. He regarded his bloody message, scrawled on the wall of his chamber, and wondered why the humans didn't resist, didn't insist that their leaders stop the war. He had never understood humans and so let the matter drop from his mind.

With the snow no longer covering the ground the damage to the zoo was once again much in evidence. The once grand buildings, built in Oriental or Indian or Neo-classical style but now burnt, toppled ruin, were a stark reminder of the raids from the previous autumn. In typical human bravado (or was it simply subterfuge?) these ruined edifices were decorated from top to bottom with the red, white and black banner, with the hooked cross, symbol of Phi-ra. It was almost as if the buildings, too, were being rewarded for their own destruction like the maimed soldiers who filed past. Only the mammoth building to the north of the zoo remained unchanged; massive, cold and imposing, it loomed over the horizon like a sentry, scanning the skies for any sign of the attackers.

***

More zoo gossip reached Siam late in the summer. Who started the gossip and how they came to hear of it in the first place Siam did not know. He had stopped worrying himself over such things long ago and was, in fact, inclined to regard trivial gossip as unworthy of his attention. But this news struck him as a good omen: invading armies from the west, so the gossip went, had landed in a place called France and were pushing the armies of his captors back.

Surely, Siam thought, this would mean the end of the war.

When further news later that summer came that a group of men had tried to kill the leader of the army Siam saw this, too, as a good omen. Finally, it appeared, the humans had resisted and, if the leader of the human army was dead, the war would have to end. Unfortunately, as these bits of gossip slowly turned into old news, the war continued and the wounded soldiers continued to file past, like some sad funeral cortege. The only bright side to this period was that the attacks from the air had ceased, allowing the inhabitants of the zoo to get much needed sleep. One night, after drifting off to sleep, Siam again dreamed that he was back in his native land, walking through the jungle. As in his earlier dream, he was accompanied by his mother, sister and aunts.

"Where is Kalifa the Second?" he asked his mother. "Where is the little girl?"

Siam's mother didn't reply, and smiled at him.

A movement in the brush behind Siam caused him to turn but, instead of Kalifa the Second, a tiger emerged. He recoiled a bit, realizing that, unless he did something foolish, the tiger could not harm him. The tiger smiled, showing its sharp teeth and slowly circled the bull.

"What do you want?" he demanded of the tiger.

Without a word the tiger leapt upon Siam's back but, before he could react, was surprised to see the cat turn into the little girl from his first dream.

"Kalifa the Second?" he asked, startled.

"Hello, Siam," she replied, stroking his head. "How are you?"

He explained to Kalifa the Second the situation, quickly blurting out everything about the raids and the deaths of the other elephants.

"I know all about that," she replied.

In a flash she was standing in front of him, her feet firmly on the ground.

"But, how…" Siam faltered.

"They are all here, you know," said Kalifa the Second.

"Where?" asked Siam, excitement in his voice. "Can I see them?"

The little girl's face curled into a mischievous smile and her brown eyes danced in the sunlight.

"Not yet," she said.

"When?" asked Siam. "When can I see Taku the Second and the others?"

"You will know when the time is right," she replied.

"Is this the place of water?" he asked.

"This is the place after," she replied.

The cryptic message awakened Siam with a start. Was this the place his grandmother and mother had mentioned when he was a child? Frustrated, he tried to force himself back to sleep in an attempt to revisit the dream, but could not.

***

As always, the crows returned to the zoo in the eleventh month but, this time, their numbers were greatly diminished and the once great, squawking black and white mass was now nothing more than a few pathetic specimens. Those who did appear quickly dropped from exhaustion in the early snow, hungry and unable to fly on, dying an ignoble death where they landed. Siam was relieved when Yach, haggard and irritable but as boisterous as ever, appeared in the courtyard.

"Goff is dead," he announced without preamble.

Sad to hear that Yach was once again a bachelor, Siam offered his condolences. Yach shook his head, a sad, far-away look in his eyes.

"No matter," he replied. "I'll not return from the summering grounds this year."

He laughed upon seeing the expression on Siam's face.

"I'm getting old," he said, "It is my time."

Siam didn't know what to say to such a pronouncement and scooted cast aside bits of melon and squash toward the crow.

"Thank you," Yach said.

As he ate he complained about the war. Their winter nesting grounds in the city were gone, he said, trees uprooted, rooftop perches blown away and there was no food to feed the freezing flock. Even if they were able to find a place to rest, he continued, the explosions drove them away. That was what had happened to poor Goff, who, in frenzy, had flown straight into a burning building. He shook his head.

Again Siam found no words to comfort his old friend. He, too, had been disappointed when the attacks had resumed but at least he had a place to sleep, with plenty of food, even in the midst of the chaos. Yach seemed to relish the news, however, that the armies of the east were winning, pressing the humans further and further west. Soon, he said, they would be in Berlin and the war would be finished. Siam didn't know whether or not to believe this news. So many times in the past he had thought that the war was surely about to end, why should this be any different?

"Trust me," said Yach, "the armies from the east will be here soon, and then the war will be over."

Finally, his appetite sated, Yach wished Siam a long life and flew off into the darkening sky. As a farewell to the ugly tower, which continued to dominate the sky, the old crow swooped at the human figures atop it and disappeared.

Chapter Fifteen

1945

The winter was harsh, and a blizzard coated everything in deep snow, adding not only to the animal's misery but to their human keepers, too, who were forced into the inclement weather to care for their charges. Braving snow and ice and the occasional attack, the humans punctually brought food and water to the zoo's remaining animals, somehow managing to keep the feedings on schedule. Despite their obvious dedication, Siam remained aggressive and refused to allow the humans to enter his cage, even when they came bearing gifts of food. He took a perverse satisfaction in watching them shiver as they stood in the ice and sleet, carefully placing the hay and fruits in his cage, cautious of the aggressive bull. Pongo, the gorilla, maintained an aggressive attitude, too, but mostly sat on the floor of his cage awaiting the end.

At the beginning of the second month a raid, seemingly directed at the building adjacent to the zoo, the one that housed the metal cars that moved on tracks, made it seem to Siam as if the end had finally arrived. Wave after wave of the metal birds droned overhead and the resulting explosions shook the ground and rained down dust and burning paper on the zoo. The tower to the north fired into the air, searching for the attackers, their guns making a thump, thump, thump noise that caused the snow on the ground to shudder. Siam stood in his cage and once again raged at the sky, at the attackers at the goddess. The walls of his enclosure shuddered with each blast and he was convinced that this, finally, would be the end. But it was not, and another big raid took place near the end of the month and the attackers returned night after night, their objective a mystery to the elephant. Clearly the city around him was already in ruins, so why should the attackers continue to return night after night when it appeared that their work was done? The only obvious answer was that the attacker's objective could only have been a psychological one. Not that he pretended to understand the humans and their thirst for war, this could never be. But his instinct told him that he was right, that the bombings would continue until every animal and human in the city was insane.

By the fourth month the bombings had, inexplicably, ceased. The first flowers of spring had begun to poke through the torn and desecrated earth as if in defiance of the destruction around them. Birds had reappeared, too, whether returning from their wintering grounds in the south or simply emerging in the absence of bombs, Siam didn't know. Still, he was happy to hear their innocent chatter in the remaining trees, even the return of the sparrows. With these pleasant diversions, however, came the inevitable reminders of war. For one thing, the humans had begun to scrawl cryptic messages on the sides of the zoo buildings. One, scrawled on the wall of the nearby hippo house in black paint by two young boys dressed like soldiers, confounded Siam. Though he could not read the human language, he studied the message closely, as if this could help him understand.

"Berlin bleibt deutsche!"

Obviously, Siam decided after long consideration, it was a call to arms. Perhaps Yach had been right, perhaps the enemy was poised to take the city from his captors. What such a possibility meant for him and the other animals Siam couldn't guess but, by the middle of the fourth month, the water supply to the zoo was shut off along with the electricity. The electricity really only affected the humans, so Siam didn't care. But a lack of water meant deprivation of a vital necessity to the hippos in the neighboring cage. Rosa cried and complained of her dried and peeling skin and Siam was truly sorry for her, Zuzana and the baby, Knautschke.

"Stay strong, Rosa," he called across the moat. "I'm sure that they will turn the water back on soon."

"I hope so," groaned Rosa. "My skin itches so badly."

But that very day bombs once again rained down upon the zoo. These bombs, however, didn't appear to fall from the sky and there was no sign of the metal birds. These bombs, inexplicably, seemed to come from the neighboring park and exploded on the zoo grounds randomly. Soldiers, old men and boys, their faces dirty and tired, scrambled to and fro. There was much disagreement among the animals as to what was happening and, during a lull in the attacks, Siam was surprised the see the zoo director, haggard and unshaven, standing at his cage. In his hand he held one of the long weapons that the other humans had used to kill his mother, and he was joined by thee man with the iron rod. The two humans spoke at length, now and then looking at the elephant, but finally left. Small pops could be heard here and there and Siam peered from his cage, afraid to emerge. Aside from the popping sounds, the zoo was strangely quiet. Finally, the popping sounds stopped and Siam fell into a fitful sleep. An hour later, however, he was awakened by a familiar voice. He opened his eyes and saw Charlie standing outside his cage, peering in at the sleeping elephant. On his right hand was a white bandage and, without a word, Charlie unwrapped the soot stained bandage, revealing that his hand had been removed at the wrist.

"They took it," he said, searching Siam's face.

"Get in here!" ordered the elephant. "Hurry, before they see you!"

Without further prodding, Charlie scampered into the elephant's cage and hid behind one of Siam's massive legs.

Siam turned his head to look at his friend. Although he was deeply saddened by the loss of Charlie's hand, his sudden reappearance filled him with a renewed sense of happiness. Besides, he reasoned, the hand had been horribly disfigured by fire. Perhaps this was the only option open to the humans. Nevertheless, an elephant couldn't know what it was like for an ape to lose a hand. It could have been similar to an elephant losing a trunk, for all Siam knew, so he offered his apologies.

"I'm sorry about your hand," he said. "Does it hurt much?"

Charlie nodded and looked up at the elephant with pleading eyes. The skin from Charlie's forearm had been pulled tightly over the stump and stitches crisscrossed the end of it.

"Now I can't climb," he said, holding the stump up for Siam to see.

"You climbed well enough with your injured hand," replied Siam. "You will manage without it. Besides," he added his tone softer, "you're here now and I will take care of you."

Charlie nodded, a sad smile creeping across his tiny face. Without another word he walked to the corner, where hay was stacked, and crawled atop, where he fell into a quick sleep. When he awakened a few hours later, he told Siam of the atrocities that were being perpetrated by the humans at the zoo. In an effort to make sure that no animals escaped from their cages during the attacks, the humans had decided to kill any threatening animals beforehand. Lions, tigers, panthers and hyenas were all killed in their cages, rather than allowing for the risk of their escape. Charlie had personally witnessed the killing of the lone baboon as he sat in his cage.

"It was terrible," he recounted to Siam. "The zoo director placed his rifle to the great ape's head and the ape pushed the gun away. Once more the zoo director aimed but the ape, still calmly sitting in his cage, pushed it away again. The third time he fired and the ape fell over dead."

Tiny tears filled Charlie's eyes.

"That's when I escaped again," he concluded.

Siam was speechless and wondered if Charlie's story explained the strange visit to his own cage by the zoo director. Obviously, they had considered killing him, too.

"We're safe now," said Siam, although he wasn't sure if this was true or not.

Charlie looked at the now faded script on the wall.

"That is my elephant name," said Siam, reading his friend's face. "What is your ape name?"

Charlie looked confused and shrugged and Siam understood.

"You were born here?" he asked the monkey.

Charlie slowly nodded his head.

That night, as he peered into the darkness, Siam saw the eye of Ha, looking down upon him. Her eye was half closed, half open, giving the impression that the goddess was unhappy, angry even. Siam turned away from the half orb in the sky. Perhaps, he thought, Ha was not happy about what was happening, after all. Perhaps now she would end the misery and destroy their human captors. Smoke occasionally obscured the goddess, sometimes red sometimes orange, other times green.

"Goddess, please," he said, turning his face back to the sky, "if you are truly angry at what you see then free us from this place."

He looked at the sleeping monkey, who was curled in a ball in the corner and twitched as if dreaming. Once Charlie's movements had ceased, and he seemed peacefully at sleep, Siam continued.

"And not just me, goddess," he whispered. "Charlie, too, and all of the animals here…free us."

When the goddess gave no reply, Siam walked back to the corner but could not rest.

***

Two days later, the pair was awakened from an uncertain sleep by the sounds of more explosions, these much closer and on the zoo grounds. Charlie rushed to Siam and cowered behind one of the elephant's legs.

"Get on top of me!" yelled Siam.

He was afraid that, in his own panic, he might step on the tiny ape. Charlie hesitated a moment but, as Siam jumped to the sounds of more explosions, suddenly understood. Siam didn't wait for Charlie to comply, however, at grabbed the monkey, placing him squarely on his head. The tower outside the zoo's walls had retrained its massive guns and was now firing down toward the city. Massive shells flew through the air and the skies around the elephant house turned into fire brighter than the sun. The ground shook with each explosion and bits of masonry and tile became airborne as shots found their targets. Humans ran past the elephant house, their heads low, running from the invaders. One, a human child, was struck and fell. His lifeless body rolled into the moat. The sound of a great explosion pierced the air and, in a flash, Siam saw that the hippo house had been hit. Knautschke screamed for his mother but Rosa and Zuzana were both silent, killed by the bombs.

"Knautschke!" screamed Siam, afraid to leave his cage, "get inside!"

The frightened baby hippo dutifully complied as more explosions shook the ground nearby. Siam peered out into the thin, early morning light and saw movement.

Suddenly, from the zoo entrance, new machines appeared. They were machines that Siam had never seen. To Siam they resembled mechanical elephants, made of steel and on wheels. They even had what looked like erect, metal trunks protruding from their faces. Their trunks, however, did not shoot water but flame.

"Phi-ra!" exclaimed Siam.

Three of the metal beasts rolled into the zoo, followed closely by humans in different uniforms than those of his human captors. These uniforms were baggy, brown uniforms and these new humans paid little attention to Siam as they passed by. One of the metal beasts stopped beside the hippo house and began firing at the tower outside the zoo's walls. Unfortunately, this had little effect on the tower and it returned fire, obliterating the metal beast. To Siam's amazement, humans, engulfed in flames, emerged from within the beast and fell to the ground dead. The other machines continued firing at the tower, however, and were quickly joined by others.

Suddenly, an ocelot, looking scared out of its wits, darted past the elephant house. As the little cat dodged the explosions around it, Siam heard it nervously lamenting the loss of a place called Paraguay. The poor creature turned a corner and disappeared from sight. Charlie, who had somehow managed to stay atop Siam's head, screamed uncontrollably.

"Let's get out of here," he said.

"No," argued Siam. "We're much safer in here. If we go out there we will be killed."

Charlie didn't seem to hear or, perhaps, didn't want to hear. He jumped from Siam's back and ran to the rear of the cage.

"Come on," he said, stepping easily through the bars.

Bullets zipped through the air and struck the nearby fence.

"Charlie," implored Siam, "please get back here."

Another explosion roared nearby. Frightened, Charlie retreated back into the cage.

"We can't stay here," he said.

"It's safer than out there," argued Siam. "The walls will protect us."

Another explosion seemed to tell him otherwise, however, and, before Siam could argue any further, Charlie disappeared into the midst of the battle. Siam's screams for the monkey to return were drowned out by the sounds of the guns and he grew quiet, leaning against the wall for support.

By the first week of the fifth month the guns finally fell silent and the defenders of the tower surrendered to the attackers. The war, it seemed, had finally ended. News of deaths found its way to Siam. Pongo, the gorilla, it was said, had been stabbed to death, along with a chimpanzee, by the invaders. Rosa and Zuzana were, of course, dead, killed by the shelling. Of the more than three thousand animals, who had once lived in the zoo, rumor went, only ninety-one survived, including Siam, Abu, the stork, Knautschke and Suse, the chimpanzee. Though he inquired tirelessly, Siam never discovered Charlie's fate. Like the frightened ocelot, which had passed the elephant enclosure during the shelling, he had simply vanished.

Chapter Sixteen

1947

An entire year had passed since the end of the war and Siam, only twenty-six seasons old, felt as if he had lived sixty seasons. He and the other animals had survived a total of three hundred and fourteen raids on the city, along with shelling and tank battles. He, as with so many of the other zoo's animals, was simply tired.

Shortly after the end of the battle clean up began at the zoo; the destroyed weapons, the metal beasts and burned out lorries were hauled off, along with the dead bodies of humans and animals alike. Holes formed from explosions were filled in and destroyed enclosures were either patched up or razed altogether. Many buildings, like the destroyed aquarium, sat untouched, a burnt out shell for the whole first year.

The victorious attackers placed armed sentries outside of each of the cages, something that had at first confounded Siam but, when he spied humans cutting up a dead horse a few days after the end of the fighting, he understood. They were starving and, without the protection of this new army, he and the surviving animals would be killed.

Dog food.

The previous fall had been difficult with many food shortages in the zoo, yet Siam had managed to subsist on the meager rations available. The baby hippo, Knautschke, was lonely and cried at night for his mother. Although his mood was foul, Siam couldn't help but pity the orphaned hippo. Despite the difference of their species, they shared much, most of all their imprisonment but also the deaths of their mothers. But Knautschke had been born in the zoo, Siam reminded himself, so, much like Wastl, freedom wouldn't mean much to the baby hippo.

The crows, their numbers diminished by the war, had returned that previous fall, too. As he had himself predicted, Yach was not among them. A young crow, which Siam approached, had rudely informed Siam that he had never heard of Yach before and he was quickly driven away by an older bird, who screamed at the youngster for not respecting his elders. His lecture over, he turned to Siam.

"Yach has gone away to Summerland," he told the elephant, "he is now at peace."

"I am sorry to hear that," replied Siam. "What news from the Munich zoo?"

The crow shook his head. The Munich zoo, too, had been bombed. The elephants Matadi, Shari, Adam and Tembo had all died. Siam was shocked to hear of the death of sweet Tembo but, it was the next revelation which shocked him even more. The crow explained that Seppl, too, had died after escaping, shot dead by the zoo director.

Siam reeled at the bad news. Just as Wastl had been killed by the zoo director in Berlin, his brother, Seppl, had been killed by the zoo director's brother in Munich. Siam pressed the crow, certain that he had confused the two stories, but the crow screeched his objections, insisting that he was certain his story was correct.

Siam apologized for having voiced doubt and thanked the crow for the news.

***

A year.

Left foot.

A year.

Right foot.

A year.

Left foot.

Siam repeated this over and over, rocking listlessly from his right foot to his left. A year had passed and he was still in his cage. Why? Why had the humans not freed him and the other animals when the war ended? Why had the goddess not answered his prayers? The humans returned to the zoo in droves, though relatively few were civilians. The new visitors wore all manner of uniform and spoke in a variety of human languages, none of which Siam could comprehend. The few of the original humans that did return, the ones in the fancy uniforms of the early days, no longer wore their uniforms and looked relieved that the whole mess was behind them. And, although Siam couldn't comprehend the reasoning, the zoo director remained at his post, despite the mess he had made of the zoo and despite all of the animals that had perished under his care.

By spring, activity outside the zoo's walls provided a welcome bit of entertainment for Siam. The gigantic tower, it appeared, was to be destroyed. The big guns that had been mounted on the roof of the great monolith were removed as was anything that might have been useful to the victors. Siam watched the dismantling of the structure with happiness; he had never liked it in the first place and, now that it was to be destroyed, he felt vindicated in his dislike for it. But even the diversion created by the destruction of the tower could not assuage Siam's desperate loneliness, the feeling that he had been deserted by everyone.

He stood in the center of his cage, day after day, slowly rocking back and forth on his front feet, bored and lonely.

He ate what little food was available, but had developed a bad case of diarrhea, accompanied by abdominal cramps that made it nearly impossible to move. Siam suspected that the moldy straw the humans had been feeding him was to blame but, as it was all he had to eat, he had little choice but to accept it.

Summer was coming, Siam could feel it but, in his melancholy, he didn't care. Most of all he longed to be free, free from the discomfort he felt, free from his loneliness, free, once and for all from the damned zoo. To be somewhere, anywhere that he wasn't standing in his own shit would have been paradise. He looked at his scrawled message on the wall, now faded, the blood a faint, rusty brown, and laughed.

"I am Da-ra," he whispered, enjoying his secret rebellion.

A small mouse crept across the ground, picking at bits of hay and, for some reason, the little creature's presence angered him. He remembered the old human with the yellow star, the one who had shared his peanuts with him and the way the mice had stolen the peanuts that fell into the moat. Enraged, Siam picked up the little creature and tossed him against the concrete wall of the elephant house. The mouse fell to the ground dead and Siam, snapped from his rage, realized what he had done. With tears in his eyes he rushed to the tiny body and tenderly retrieved it from its resting place.

"I'm sorry," he whispered, cradling the mouse in his bent trunk. "Please forgive me."

Siam didn't know if he was addressing the dead rodent or the goddess. He remembered the stories of the goddess, the ones his mother had taught him as a child.

Because she couldn't bear to leave her creations without protection and fearing that Phi-ra might plot his revenge, Ha decided to keep watch over them from the cover of the nighttime sky, where she remains cloaked, one of her eyes, luminous and white, watching her children from the heavens. There she remains as mother protector and lady of the cold months.

Was the goddess still watching him? Siam didn't know any longer but had to believe. He cocked his head toward the sky.

"Please forgive me," he repeated. "Take me from this place…to the place after."

That night, feeling particularly sick and with a raging fever, Siam drifted into an uneasy sleep. The dead mouse remained where he had placed it upon his back. When he awakened he was back in the jungle. He looked around but saw no other elephants. Suddenly, to his right, he saw movement. Emerging from the lush grass was an elephant bigger than ant he had ever seen and her gold skin shimmered in the sunlight. Although he had never seen her, no elephant had, he knew that this was Gro, the first elephant. On her back was Kalifa the Third, in the form of the human girl child, and in Kalifa the Third's arms was the monkey, Charlie.

Siam bowed before Gro and placed the tip of his trunk in her mouth in homage.

"Arise, my son," she replied. "I demand no worship from you."

Siam lifted his head and regarded Kalifa the Third. She smiled at him, a coquettish gleam in her brown eyes.

"We knew you were coming," she said. "Charlie told me."

"But, how could Charlie know?" he asked, confused.

Kalifa the Second laughed at the question and Charlie scampered onto Siam's back. Gro began to walk in the direction of the jungle, Kalifa the Second at her side and Siam followed.

"Where are we going?" he asked, trying to keep step with the much larger elephant.

"To see the others," replied Kalifa the Second.

"The others?" asked Siam.

Again, Kalifa the Second merely giggled in response to Siam's question but, as they came to a rise overlooking a great valley, Siam saw a herd of elephants milling about below them. This time it was not only his mother and aunts and sisters that Siam saw. Standing among the elephants was Toni the Third, Mary, Mampe, Wastl and Taku the Second.

Siam could feel his heart racing and he looked at Kalifa the Second, his face expectant.

"If this is not the place of water, what is it?" he asked.

"This is the place after," she replied with a laugh, "the place after eternal sleep."

"Is this real?" he asked.

This time Kalifa the Second didn't laugh and her face was serious.

"It is your time, Siam," she said. "The goddess has brought you here, as you wished."

Siam studied the girl's face for a moment and then, with a loud trumpet, charged down the hill to join his long lost family.

He was finally free from the zoo.

Author's Note

Although this is a work of fiction, all of the animals listed in this book are real. While some details of their story have been manipulated for the sake of story telling, they all existed. For example, Siam was never at the Munich zoo but was transferred to Berlin directly from the Circus Krone in Munich. Additionally, there is no evidence that Siam and Taku II were ever coupled. Again, this detail was added merely in the interest of telling a story. And, while the character of the old man with a beard appeared wearing the Star of David in 1940, this probably couldn't have actually occurred until a year later. Much else is true, however: the British and Americans did bomb the zoo numerous times, just as the German Luftwaffe had bombed zoos in Rotterdam, Warsaw and elsewhere. The story of the air raid of 22-23 November 1943 is historically accurate as is my description of the destruction of the animal houses on that night. The gorilla, Pongo, was in fact found stabbed to death in his cage. While the details of his death remain elusive, it is generally believed that attacking Russian soldiers were responsible, although it should be mentioned that three dead SS soldiers were found in front of his cage. A final point is the odd manner in which the brothers, Wastl and Seppl died. Though it sounds like fiction, both were shot escaping, Wastl by Lutz Heck in Berlin and Seppl by Heinz Heck, Lutz's brother, in Munich. Knautschke, the hippo, is the true success story here; not only was the little hippo born during the air raid of 22 November 1943, but he survived the conflagration and went on to sire future generations of hippos at the Berlin and Leipzig zoos, siring thirty descendants in all. He died at the Berlin zoo in 1988 at the age of forty-five. Two elephants mentioned in this story also survived the war. Stasi, Wastl and Seppl's sister and the daughter of Boy and Cora, died at the age of thirty-four at the Munich zoo in 1968 and Omar, the father of Indra and Orje, died at the age of thirty-eight at the Leipzig zoo in 1957. Siam's death, at the age of twenty-six, was listed as having been caused by enteritis, an inflammation of the intestines.

The flak tower outside the zoo's walls was finally destroyed in 1948 and the elephant gate at Number Nine Budapest Street, destroyed in the fighting of 1944-45, has since been rebuilt to its former glory.

Appendix

List of elephants at the Berlin Zoo during the Second World War:

Name/Species/Sex	Birth Status	At the Berlin Zoo	Death/Cause
Siam-Asian Male	Wild born 1921	1933-1947	Enteritis
Wastl-Asian Male	Captive born-1932	1939-1943	Shot escaping bombs
Orje-Asian Male	Captive born-1936	1936-1938	Infection
Harry-Asian Male	Wild born-1880	1905-1934	Unknown cause
Taku II-Asian Female	Wild born-date?	1938-1943	Allied bombings
Aida-Asian Female	Wild born-1923	1935-1943	Allied bombings
Indra-Asian Female	Captive born-1938	1938-1943	Allied bombings
Birma-Asian Female	Wild born 1930	1936-1943	Allied bombings
Toni III-Asian Female	Wild born-1905	1932-1943	Allied bombings
Jenny II-Asian Female	Wild born-1911	1938-1943	Allied bombings
Kalifa II-Asian Female	Captive born-1928	1928-1939	Infection from cuts
Korat-Asian Female	Wild born-1932	1935-1938	Unknown cause
Taku-Asian Female	Wild born-1932	1934-1938	Unknown cause
Toni II (Mary) Asian Female	Wild born-1903	1925-1934	"Accident"

Lindi-African Female	Wild born-1920	1935-1943	Allied bombings
Carl-African Male	Wild born 1921	1924-1935	Intestinal Disease
Mampe-African Male	Wild born-1917	1926-1933	Unknown cause

Sources

"Berlin's Last Elephant," Life Magazine, October 15, 1945, (page 42).

O'Donnell, James P, "The Bunker". Houghton Mifflin, 1978.

Ryan, Cornelius, "The Last Battle". Simon and Schuster, 1966.

Read, Anthony, "The Fall of Berlin". Da Capo Press, 1995.

Internet

www.elephant.se/location2.php?location_id=20 Extensive information online regarding elephants kept at the Berlin zoo, including breeds and dates of birth and death.

www.raf.mod.uk Extensive information online regarding the bombing of Berlin, including the Bomber Command Campaign Diary, weather conditions, etc.

Acknowledgments

Special thanks to Dan Koehl, elephant keeper at Kolmarden Zoo in Sweden and webmaster of www.elephant.se for sharing his knowledge regarding the Berlin Zoo's elephants, particularly the elephant known as Mary.

About the Author

Curtis Christopher Comer is a freelance writer, columnist and animal lover who lives in St. Louis with his partner, Tim. His most recent book, (Not Quite) Out to Pasture, is available from Walrus Publishing.